ONE GIRL HOLDS
THE FATE OF THE UNIVERSE
IN HER HANDS.

the

OF HARUHI SUZUMIYA

boredom

NAGARU TANIGAWA

LITTLE, BROWN AND COMPANY
NEW YORK BOSTON

Yen Press

Suzumiya Haruhi No Taikutsu copyright © Nagaru TANIGAWA 2004
Edited by KADOKAWA SHOTEN
First published in Japan in 2004 by KADOKAWA CORPORATION, Tokyo
English translation rights arranged with KADOKAWA CORPORATION, Tokyo,
through TUTTLE-MORI AGENCY, INC., Tokyo.

English translation by Chris Pai for MX Media LLC

English translation © 2010 by Hachette Book Group, Inc.

Little, Brown and Company

Hachette Book Group
1290 Avenue of the Americas, New York, NY 10104
Visit our website at www.lb-teens.com
www.jointhesosbrigade.com

Little, Brown and Company is a division of
Hachette Book Group, Inc.
The Little, Brown name and logo are
trademarks of Hachette Book Group, Inc.

First U.S. Edition: July 2010

Library of Congress Cataloging-in-Publication Data

Tanigawa, Nagaru.
[Suzumiya Haruhi no taikutsu. English]
The boredom of Haruhi Suzumiya / Nagaru Tanigawa ; [English translation by Chris Pai]. — 1st U.S. ed.
p. cm.
ISBN 978-0-316-03886-7 (hc) / 978-0-316-03887-4 (pb)
[1. Supernatural—Fiction. 2. Clubs—Fiction. 3. High schools—Fiction. 4. Schools—Fiction. 5. Japan—Fiction.] I. Pai, Chris. II. Title.

PZ7.T16139Bo 2010
[Fic]—dc22

2009042692

10 9 8 7 6 5 4 3 2

RRD-C

Printed in the United States of America

the

OF HARUHI SUZUMIYA

boredom

NAGARU TANIGAWA

First released in Japan in 2003, *The Melancholy of Haruhi Suzumiya* quickly established itself as a publishing phenomenon, drawing much of its inspiration from Japanese pop culture and Japanese comics in particular. With this foundation, the original publication of each book in the Haruhi series included several black-and-white spot illustrations as well as a four-page color insert—all of which are faithfully reproduced here to preserve the authenticity of the first-ever English edition.

PROLOGUE

Looking back, the memorable inauguration of the SOS Brigade, which had left me, not Haruhi, in a state of melancholy, had been back in the beginning of spring, and the incident involving the production of the independent film, which, naturally, had forced me, not Haruhi, to sigh, had technically happened in autumn if you go by the calendar.

Approximately half a year had passed in between, of course, and Haruhi sure wasn't going to sit around and watch six whole months, including all of summer, pass by. Naturally, it goes without saying that we ended up involved in various irrational and incomprehensible events or pseudo-events that shouldn't even be called as such.

At any rate, the season was what it was, and baffling ideas were popping out of Haruhi's head the way insects pop out when the temperature rises. I could live with the popping-out part, but the fact of the matter was, we would be forced to deal with whatever idea had popped out. Seriously, what's up with that?

I have no idea how Koizumi, Nagato, and Asahina felt about all this, but my subjective symptoms told me, at least, that while my energy and strength remained at adequate levels, I always ended up feeling like a little round animal that couldn't move after eating more than it should have, leaving no choice but to roll down the hill.

I may still be rolling at this very moment.

After all, Haruhi has a habit that other people would find excruciatingly annoying of thinking about utterly worthless things whenever her head isn't filled with happy thoughts. Basically, it would appear that she's unable to tolerate any situation which requires her to do nothing. She's the kind of person who will forcibly find something to do when no such thing exists. And based on my experience, we can no longer have peace of mind once Haruhi opens her mouth. And we may never have it again. She's unbelievable.

Haruhi Suzumiya, the girl who hates boredom above all else, regardless of the good or the bad.

And so I would like to take this opportunity to fill you in on the various undertakings of the SOS Brigade to counter the boredom during the six months when melancholy turned to sigh. I can't really explain how this constitutes an opportunity, but it won't kill me to talk about it, and it'd be pretty satisfying to get it all off my chest and share this indescribable feeling with someone else.

Let's see...I'll start from the stupid baseball tournament.

CONTENTS

THE BOREDOM OF HARUHI SUZUMIYA

One day in the "Save the world by Overloading it with fun Haruhi Suzumiya Brigade," or SOS Brigade, hideout (which was technically still the literary club room), Haruhi made the following loud announcement, sounding very much like the captain of a high school baseball team that had drawn the top seed at nationals.

"We're entering the baseball tournament!"

It was after school one day in June. Two weeks after the nightmare-esque incident that had rendered me unable to focus on my studies. Consequently, I was facing my midterm results, the real nightmare, in early summer.

On the other hand, Haruhi, who didn't listen to a word in class regardless of how attentive she appeared, managed to score in the top ten for our year. If there is a god in this world, he or she has horrible judgment and a nasty sense of humor.

… Well, none of that really matters. The issue right now would be Haruhi's announcement.

What did she just say?

I looked around at the faces of the other three people in the room.

The first one to catch my eye was the baby face of Mikuru Asahina, the upperclassman who looked like she was in middle school. An incredibly adorable girl who looked ready to fly up into the heavens if you were to attach white wings to her back. And I am also aware that she has a dynamite body unbefitting her face and petite stature.

For some reason, Asahina, the only person in the room not wearing the high school uniform, was garbed in a light pink nurse outfit as she stared at Haruhi with her lovely lips slightly parted. She's dressed as a nurse not because she's a nursing student or a costume-wearing fanatic, but simply because Haruhi ordered it. She must have bought it off some shady Internet site again. Haruhi brought the costume and forced Asahina to put it on. Any person would wonder, "What is the purpose of this?" Allow me to answer.

"There isn't any."

At one point, Haruhi had delivered the decree, "You must always wear this outfit when you're in the club room!" and Asahina had responded, "Y-You can't be serious…," while in tears, yet she obediently followed orders, even when passing out club flyers to the whole school. She's so sweet that I just want to run up to her and give her a hug, though I haven't done so yet. I swear.

Incidentally, her standard attire two weeks ago had been a maid outfit, and that maid outfit was currently on a hanger in the corner of the club room. The maid's one is cuter and suits her better, plus it matches my tastes, so I'm hoping she returns to her roots soon. Asahina would probably grant my request. While acting all flustered and embarrassed. Yeah, I like it.

And after hearing Haruhi's announcement concerning baseball, Asahina, currently a nurse, responded.

"What...?"

She reacted in a voice as lovely as a canary chirping before falling silent. An understandable reaction.

Next, I turned my gaze to the other girl in the room.

Yuki Nagato was about as tall as Asahina, but if you were to compare how much they stood out, it'd be like comparing horsetails to sunflowers. As usual, she appeared to be oblivious to everything going on around her as her eyes were firmly locked on the pages of her thick hardcover. Her fingers would move to turn the page every ten seconds or so, and you would finally know she was still alive. You could probably get more chatter out of a parakeet that knew Japanese and more movement out of a hamster in hibernation.

It doesn't really make a difference whether she's here or not, so there isn't much point in spending effort on a thorough explanation, but I suppose I should at least try to introduce her. She's a first-year, just like Haruhi and me, and the only member of the literary club that originally occupied this club room. In other words, our student association known as the SOS Brigade is renting this room, or it's more like we're parasites who've turned this room into our stronghold. Naturally, we still haven't been recognized by the school. The charter application I turned in a while back was refused by the student council.

"..."

I turned away from the apathetic Nagato to find the grinning handsome face of Itsuki Koizumi next to her. He looked at me with an amused expression on his face. It pisses me off for no real reason. This guy's less relevant than Nagato. The mysterious transfer student—except that Haruhi's the only one who calls him mysterious—brushed aside his bangs and that annoyingly good-looking face broke into a smile. Our eyes met and he shrugged so naturally I wanted to beat him down. Does he want me to beat him down?

"What are we entering?"

Nobody else reacted, so as usual, I reluctantly posed the question. Why does everyone want to treat me like Haruhi's interpreter? I don't think you could find a more painful role.

"Here."

Haruhi triumphantly handed me a flyer. As I noted Asahina, who had nothing but bad memories when it came to flyers, covertly huddling up out of the corner of my eye, I read the flyer out loud.

"The Ninth City Amateur Baseball Tournament is seeking participants."

This town apparently holds a single-elimination tournament to determine a champion baseball team. The event is organized by government officials so it's an officially sponsored annual event with a lot of history.

"Hmm…"

I muttered as I looked up. Haruhi's bright shining face was 100 percent smile and practically touching me. I reflexively took half a step back.

"So, who's entering this baseball tournament?"

I already knew the answer, but I asked anyway.

"We are, obviously!" Haruhi declared.

"Does your 'we' include Asahina, Nagato, Koizumi, and me?"

"Of course!"

"Do we have a say in this?"

"We'll need to find four more people."

As always, she hears only what she wants to hear. I suddenly thought of something.

"Do you know the rules for baseball?"

"I have a general idea. It's a sport where you throw, hit, run, slide, tackle, all that good stuff. I joined the baseball team for a bit so I know the basics."

4

"How many days were you on the baseball team?"

"A little under an hour, I think. But it was dead boring so I left immediately."

"So why do we have to participate in a baseball tournament if you found it dead boring?"

Haruhi's response to this obvious question was as follows:

"It's a chance to make ourselves known across the land, Kyon. If we win this tournament, it may be the spark which will eventually allow the SOS Brigade name to stand on its own. A golden opportunity."

I would prefer that the name of this brigade not spread any more than it already has. Besides, what's the point of making the name stand on its own? How is this a golden opportunity?

I was perplexed, and Asahina was flustered, while Koizumi murmured, "I see, I see," with an unperturbed look on his face. I couldn't tell if Nagato was troubled by any of this or if she'd even been listening at all, but she had the usual stiff porcelain expression on her face.

"Right? Isn't this a nice idea, Mikuru?"

Faced with that abrupt question, Asahina panicked.

"Huh? Huh? B-B-But..."

"What is it?"

Haruhi circled around Asahina the way an alligator would approach a fawn drinking water on a riverbank and suddenly threw her arms around the bent-over, petite nurse, or hospital attendant rather, from behind.

"Wah! Wh-What are you—What are you doing...?!"

"Listen up, Mikuru. In this brigade, the leader's orders are absolute! Insubordination is a severe offense! If you have anything to say, we'll listen to it during the meeting."

Meeting? Like those meetings that are held so she can arbitrarily force us to do stuff that makes no sense at all?

Haruhi had her arms around the struggling Asahina like an albino Japanese rat snake.

"You're okay with baseball, right? Just to be clear, we're aiming for first place! I won't accept a single loss! Because I really hate to lose!"

"Awawawa…"

Asahina trembled with her eyes darting around and her face flushed.

Haruhi, who was practically executing a sleeper hold, suddenly bit down on Asahina's ear as she glared at me. Maybe because I looked at her like I wanted to be in that sleeper hold.

"Okay?!"

Why do you care? You're just going to ignore us anyway.

"Why not?"

Koizumi voiced his agreement.

Hey, don't just cheerfully support her. Throw in an objection every once in a while.

"In that case, I'll go get equipment from the baseball team."

Haruhi shot off like a miniature tornado. The emancipated Asahina sank into a chair as Koizumi offered his interpretation.

"Aren't you relieved that we aren't capturing aliens or going on a camping trip to search for cryptids? If we're playing baseball, we shouldn't have to worry about encountering any of those unrealistic phenomena we dread."

"I guess so."

At the time, I agreed. Not even Haruhi would say that you would need aliens, time travelers, or espers to play baseball. When the alternative is to look around town for supernatural phenomena that couldn't possibly happen (that was the SOS Brigade's main activity), I'd much rather play some baseball. Plus, Asahina was bobbing her head up and down.

In hindsight, our conjecture was completely off the mark. I

could have lived with being off the mark, but it ended up piercing the wall behind the bull's eye and flew off lord knows where, but I didn't realize any of this until later on.

Basically, in my opinion, it didn't have to be baseball. She would have been fine with whatever happened to catch her eye. First off, this not-quite-a-student-association with the embarrassing name "SOS Brigade" that still isn't recognized by the school was basically just created by Haruhi on a whim. After all, the long and frightfully conceited official name of this enigma of a brigade is the "**S**ave the world by **O**verloading it with fun Haruhi **S**uzumiya Brigade." My plan to change the name to something slightly better went to pieces unfortunately, and ever since, there hasn't been an opportunity to change it.

At one point, I had asked Haruhi what the purpose of this club was, and she'd responded with a look on her face like a foot soldier who had just killed an enemy general.

"To find aliens, time travelers, and espers and have fun with them!"

The famous words that would confirm Haruhi Suzumiya, already known in our school for her bizarre behavior, as a complete freak.

And yeah, much like how a crow goes after shiny things, how a cat instinctively jumps after anything small that rolls around, or how a person who sees a cockroach in the kitchen goes for the insecticide, anything that draws her attention, be it dodgeball, gateball, or portball, will lead to her saying, "Let's do this!" I should probably be happy that it wasn't a rugby tournament. Since that would require finding even more members.

In other words, Haruhi was bored.

I have no idea what kind of negotiations were involved, but Haruhi returned like a whirlwind carrying an assortment of baseball equipment. The cardboard box, which looked as though an abandoned puppy could fit into it, contained nine beat-up gloves, a chipped-up metal bat, and a few dirty baseballs.

"Wait."

I took a close look at the flyer again.

"This tournament uses softballs. What's the point in bringing hardballs?"

"A ball is a ball, right? They're the same. You hit it with a bat and it goes flying, guaranteed."

"The last time I played baseball was at my grade school. But I still know the difference between softballs and hardballs. Hardballs hurt more when you get hit."

"So don't get hit then."

Haruhi said it simply with a look suggesting she had no idea what I was talking about.

I gave up.

"So when is the game?"

"This Sunday."

"That's the day after tomorrow! That's way too soon."

"But I've already registered us. Ah, don't worry. I put 'SOS Brigade' for the team name. No mistakes in that department."

I felt exhausted.

"...Where do you plan on finding the other members?"

"Just grab any bored-looking people we see walking around."

She seriously meant that. And anybody who catches Haruhi's eye, with one exception, is not a normal person. The only exception would be me. And I have no intention of becoming acquainted with any more people I can't understand.

"I got it. You just sit tight. I'll find members. First off…"

I went through the boys of class 1-5 in my mind. Who would be willing to come if I asked…Only Taniguchi and Kunikida, probably.

Once I mentioned them, Haruhi responded.

"Those are fine."

She referred to her own classmates as objects.

"Better than nothing."

Everybody else would probably run away the second the name "Haruhi Suzumiya" came up. Let's see, what to do for the remaining two?

"Excuse me."

Asahina timidly raised her hand.

"If you don't mind, my friend would be…"

"Then we'll do that."

Haruhi replied instantly. Anyone works, apparently. You probably don't care since you're completely in the dark, but I'm a little worried about this. Asahina's friend? Her friend from when and where?

Asahina must have noticed the concern on my face since she turned to me.

"It's okay. She's from this age…ahem, someone I met from my class."

She said to reassure me. And then Koizumi opened his mouth.

"Then allow me to also bring a friend. In fact, I can think of an acquaintance who has expressed interest in our—"

I cut him off before he could finish. "You don't need to bring anybody. Anyone associated with you is bound to be a weirdo."

"I'll take care of it."

"If she's willing to take anyone, I have other people to turn to."

Haruhi nodded in a generous fashion. "Then let's start training."

Well, that was where the conversation was headed.

"Right now."

"Right now? Where?"

"The school field."

I could hear the soft sounds of the members of the baseball team going "Hey, batta, batta" through the open window.

By the way, I know I shouldn't just mention this out of nowhere, but the truth is that the other four people in the club room aren't ordinary humans for various reasons. Haruhi's the only one who doesn't realize what she is. The other three revealed their identities to me unsolicited and urged me to understand their situation. Their claims were so far beyond my comprehension that if my common sense were to be considered Earth, they would have been somewhere out past Pluto's orbit. However, after my experiences during the previous month, I had learned that apparently it was all true. I didn't really want to know that, but you could say that ever since I was included as one of Haruhi's flunkies, my wishes have had almost no chance of being granted.

Simply put, Asahina, Nagato, and Koizumi were in this school because Haruhi was. Everybody seemed to be extraordinarily concerned about Haruhi.

As far as I could tell, she was just a hyper girl, but apparently I was the only one who felt that way, and my conviction had begun to waver in recent days.

I swear. My head hasn't snapped.

The world has.

And so, I was standing on the dusty sports grounds along with the other brigade members who had strayed off the beaten track.

The members of the baseball team who had been chased out of their practice space were shooting us annoyed looks. That was to be expected. This strange group of people showed up out of nowhere, and then the leader, a girl in a sailor uniform waving a bat around, started yelling unintelligible things, leaving them dumbfounded. The next thing they knew, the baseball team's allotted space on the grounds had been occupied and they'd been ordered to fetch and toss balls. If that isn't considered annoying, I have no idea what is.

Plus our group was a bunch of people in regular school uniforms with a nurse mixed in.

"Let's start with a thousand hits!"

Per Haruhi's announcement, a rain of hits came pelting down on the bunch of us who were standing in a line near the pitcher's mound.

"Eek—"

Asahina crouched down, covering her head with her glove. I turned toward the incoming white balls, determined to prevent her from being hit. At any rate, Haruhi was sending out a real flurry of killer lasers. She's a pro at whatever she does.

Koizumi had his usual smile on his face as he blithely fielded hits.

"Indeed, it's been a long time. This brings back memories."

Koizumi bared his white teeth at me as he lightly stepped around Haruhi's wild barrage. If this is such a breeze for you, help cover Asahina.

I glanced at Nagato to find her standing erect facing forward.

She stood perfectly still, paying no attention to any balls that flew her way. She didn't even flinch when a ball passed her ear by mere millimeters. Occasionally, she would slowly move the glove on her left hand with robotic motions to catch and drop only the balls that were on a collision course with her. You could move a little more, you know. Or am I supposed to praise your dynamic visual acuity?

I probably shouldn't have been paying any attention to other people as a ball took a weird hop and grazed the bottom of my glove, landing a direct hit on Asahina's knee. What a mistake.

"Wah!"

The nurse version of Asahina shrieked.

"It hurts…"

She began sobbing. I couldn't watch anymore.

"Take care of the rest," I said to Koizumi and Nagato before I helped Asahina up and moved outside the white line.

"Hey! Where are you going?! Kyon! Mikuru! Come back here!"

"She's retiring due to injury!"

I raised one hand to counter Haruhi's protest as I took Asahina's arm and headed for the nurse's office. A much more appropriate place for her nurse outfit than the dusty club room or the rough sports grounds.

Asahina, with one hand covering her tearing eyes, apparently didn't realize I was the person she was clinging to until we were already in the hallway.

"Eek!"

She jumped away, releasing a little shriek so cute I wanted to record it, and looked up at me me with a slightly red face.

"Kyon, if you're so nice to me…it'll happen again…"

What will happen again? I shrugged.

"Asahina, you can go home now. I'll tell Haruhi that it'll take two days to recover from the hit to your leg."

"But…"

"Don't worry. It's all Haruhi's fault anyway. There's no need for you to worry."

I waved my hand. Asahina looked up at me with her face lowered. Her teary eyes made her twice as sexy.

"Thank you."

Asahina flashed me a smile so lovely my knees were buckling, as she turned back to look at me, before reluctantly walking away. Haruhi could learn a thing or two about how to behave by watching her. It'd do her a world of good.

When I returned to the sports grounds, I found that fielding practice was still going on. What amazed me was that the members of the baseball team were doing the fielding while Koizumi and Nagato stood behind the fence.

Koizumi smiled cheerfully upon spotting me.

"Why, hello there. Welcome back."

"What's she doing?"

"Exactly what it looks like. It would seem that we weren't responsive enough for her as she's been that way for a while."

She had perfect control. Every ball she hit flew exactly where she said it would.

The three of us had nothing to do as we watched Haruhi's impressive batting before that crazy girl finally set down the bat and wiped the sweat off her brow, looking satisfied. Koizumi spoke with an amused look on his face.

"Quite amazing. That was exactly one thousand hits."

"The fact that you counted to one thousand is what's amazing."

"…"

Nagato turned around in silence. I followed her lead.

"Say," I proposed to the petite, sailor uniform–garbed girl, who was turned sideways. "Could you make it rain on the day of the game? Something big enough to cancel it?"

"It is possible."

Nagato responded plainly as she continued walking.

"However, it is not recommended."

"Why's that?"

"Alterations to the local environmental data may result in aftereffects to this planet's ecosystem."

"How long will it be before these aftereffects show up?"

"Between a few centuries and ten millennia."

That won't be for a while.

"Then I guess we probably shouldn't."

"Yes."

Nagato nodded her head about five millimeters as she continued walking at a fixed pace.

I turned to look behind me and saw Haruhi, still in her school uniform, on the mound ready to begin pitching.

Two days later. Sunday. 8 AM on the dot.

We met at the city sports grounds. There were two baseball fields adjacent to the track. Each game would last five innings. The top four teams would be determined by evening, and the semifinal and final matches would be held next Sunday so it was a two-week tournament. There were many other teams around but we looked pretty out of place since our team was the only one in school gym uniforms. Almost all of the other participants were wearing baseball jerseys. And this was the first time I'd seen Nagato in something besides her school uniform, but I digress.

I found out afterward that this baseball tournament actually had some history behind it (it was only the ninth one, though) and was apparently a fairly serious competition. In that case, I wish they'd rejected Haruhi at the front desk.

By the way, a single phone call was all it had taken to garner ready consent from Taniguchi and Kunikida. Taniguchi was in it for Asahina and Nagato while Kunikida just said, "Sounds like fun," and decided to join in. Good thing they're simple-minded.

The second-year Asahina had brought along to help was named Tsuruya. A cheerful girl with hair as long as Haruhi's had been who was looking at me.

"So you're Kyon? I've heard a lot about you from Mikuru. Hmm…Heh…"

As she was talking, Asahina became noticeably flustered. What did she say about me?

And then, Haruhi was currently staring at the fourth member, brought by me.

"Kyon, come here for a second."

Haruhi dragged me to the side of the tournament's main tent with an iron grip.

"What are you thinking? You're going to have that thing play baseball?"

Thing is a bit rude now. That thing's still my sister.

"She introduced herself as a ten-year-old fifth grader. She's such a sweet little girl that it's hard to believe she's related to you. So anyway, she would do fine if this were Little League, but the baseball tournament we're entering is open to the general public!"

It's not as though I brought my sister without any thinking. This was by design, careful and thorough. Here was my logic. The fact of the matter was that I had absolutely no interest in waking up early on Sunday morning to engage in athletic activity. I had no control over the forces that had brought me to this place on this day. In which case, it would only be natural for me to want to get this over with as soon as possible. In other words, we just needed to lose fast and go on home. Considering the members we had besides my sister, we already had no chance of winning our first match. Regardless, this was Haruhi we're talking about. Watch us end up winning by accident. That would definitely be a pain. It was necessary to add a factor to guarantee our loss. With an amateur grade school girl added into the mix, it'd be a joke if we won.

I couldn't tell Haruhi, but I did, in fact, have a working human brain of my own.

"Hmph, whatever."

Haruhi snorted as she turned to the side.

"It's a good enough handicap. I'd feel bad if we slaughtered the other team."

Apparently, she is seriously intent on winning. I wonder how.

"By the way, we haven't decided on a batting order or positions yet. What are we going to do?"

"I already thought that through," Haruhi said with a satisfied smirk on her face as she took some folded-up pieces of paper out of her pocket. We just found out who our roster would be. What was she going to base her selection on?

"You don't have any problems with deciding through this, right?"

Eight lines were drawn on each sheet of paper. There were two sheets. It looked like ladder lottery to me. Maybe I was hallucinating?

"What are you talking about? It's obviously a lottery. One for batting order and one for field position. Also, I'm the pitcher and leadoff."

"...So all you came up with was the method for deciding?"

"What's with that look on your face? Got a problem with it? It's a democratic method. They used lottery to choose government officials in ancient Greece!"

Don't compare the ancient Greek government system to modern Japanese batting order selection. And you're the only one who gets to choose your own position. How is that democratic?

...Oh, well. This should mean that it'll take even less time for us to lose. When they were explaining the rules earlier, I remembered hearing that the game would be called if one team was up by ten. I should start getting ready to go home now. After all, our opponents for the first match were the three-time defending champions and the leading candidates to win this tournament.

The Kamigahara Pirates. A local college baseball team. I'd have to say that they would be considered a hardcore club. They looked dead serious. Every member was here to win. It was obvious just from watching them warm up. All of them were pumped up and shouting as they practiced throwing the ball home and setting up double plays. They were the real deal. Quite frankly, they just had a different look in their eyes. For a moment, I was starting to wonder if we were in the wrong place, before I looked at our surroundings and confirmed that we were at the city sports ground hosting the baseball tournament.

I had been fine with losing, but I was starting to want to escape reality. Our team was so pathetic that I wanted to apologize to the other team.

As I plotted how to flee in the face of the enemy, Haruhi made us all stand in a line.

"I'm going to explain our strategy now. Everybody do exactly as I say."

She sounded like a manager.

"Okay? First of all, do whatever it takes to get on base. Once you're on, steal your way to third base. Batters should hit strikes and ignore balls. Simple, right? By my calculations, we can score at least three runs an inning."

That may be what the calculations inside Haruhi's brain are saying, but I have to wonder where she gets all her confidence from. Obviously, it doesn't come from anywhere. After all, she's the very embodiment of unwarranted confidence. However, most people in this world would call such a person an "idiot." And this is no mere idiot. She reigns at the top of the food chain of the idiot world. The queen of idiots!

Allow me to inform you of the starting roster for Team SOS Brigade as determined by the god of fortune.

Leading off is pitcher Haruhi Suzumiya. Batting second is right fielder Mikuru Asahina. Batting third is center fielder Yuki Nagato. Batting cleanup is the second baseman, yours truly. Batting fifth is the left fielder, my sister. Batting sixth is catcher Itsuki Koizumi. Batting seventh is first baseman Kunikida. Batting eight is third baseman Tsuruya. Batting ninth is shortstop Taniguchi.

There you have it. No subs. No manager. No fans.

Once we had finished lining up and greeting the other team, Haruhi promptly went to the batter's box. Since we'd completely forgotten about those things called helmets, the staff lent us some secondhand white ones. As for the stuff we'd brought ourselves, there were enough yellow megaphones for the whole team courtesy of Haruhi.

Haruhi pushed up the brim of her helmet as she raised the metal bat she'd stolen from our school baseball team and flashed a cocky grin.

The umpire called for us to play ball, and the opposing team's pitcher began his windup motion.

The first pitch.

Clang.

A metallic sound rang through the air as the white ball flew a fair distance, passing over the head of the center fielder backing up furiously and hitting the fence after one hop. By the time the ball came back to the infield, Haruhi was already on second base.

I wasn't particularly surprised. I would expect Haruhi to do this well. Asahina and Koizumi probably felt the same way and I'm guessing Nagato doesn't know how to be surprised. However, the remaining members, without exception, had astonished looks on their faces as they stared at Haruhi repeatedly pumping her fist up and down. Especially the ones on the other team.

"That pitcher is totally weak! The rest of you follow my lead!" Haruhi shouted cheerfully. But it completely backfired. The opposition no longer felt like holding back just because they were facing girls.

Our second batter, Asahina, was wearing a helmet too big for her head as she nervously stood in the batter's box.

"P-Please go easy on me—Eek!"

A high inside fastball flew by before she even finished speaking. Those bastards. If you hit Asahina, there will be dire consequences. Immediate brawling.

Asahina was still as a statue as she watched the second pitch fly by. Once the umpire announced that the batter was out, she returned to the bench, noticeably relieved.

"Hey! Why aren't you swinging the bat?!"

Haruhi appears to be saying something, but we can just ignore her. All that matters is that Asahina is safe.

"..."

Our third batter was Nagato. She wordlessly walked to the batter's box, dragging the tip of the metal bat along the ground.

"..."

She let every pitch go by and was immediately struck out. She then silently returned and turned to the next batter, me.

"..."

She handed me the helmet and bat before mutely sitting down on the bench and going back to being a prop.

Haruhi's angry yelling was getting annoying. Well, it was her fault for expecting anything from Asahina and Nagato.

"Kyon! You'd better get a hit! You're batting cleanup!"

What can you possibly expect from a cleanup chosen through lottery?

I followed Nagato's lead and stood in the batter's box, without saying a word.

The first pitch I let go was a strike. I was surprised. It was pretty fast. You could even hear the swooshing sound of the ball slicing through the air. I had no idea how fast it was, but I could barely see it. In fact, I saw the pitcher throw the ball, and the next thing I knew, it was in the catcher's mitt. Haruhi doubled off a pitch like this?

The second pitch. I tried swinging. The metal bat sliced through empty air. Swing and a miss. Didn't even touch the ball. I doubt it's going to happen.

The third pitch. Whoa, the ball curved. Was that what they call a curveball? If I hadn't swung, it would have missed the outside corner and been a ball, but I swung and it was all over. Three consecutive strikeouts. Three outs. Change sides.

"Moron!"

The opposing team returned to their bench as Haruhi yelled and waved her hands from the middle-left side of the infield.

Feeling pretty ashamed.

Our defense, quite frankly, had more holes than an anthill in a savanna.

The outfield was especially horrendous. First of all, Asahina was in right field and my sister was in left and neither of them was going to be catching any fly balls. We found that out during pregame warm-ups. So when the ball flew toward right field, it was me, the second baseman, and when the ball flew toward left, it was Taniguchi, the shortstop, who had to run at full speed to where the ball was falling. Whenever Asahina saw the ball flying toward her, she would crouch down and cover her head with her glove, so we couldn't expect anything from her. My sister, on the other hand, would cheerfully run after the ball before watching it drop three meters away from where she was, so that was another lost cause.

Nagato, in center, fielded the ball perfectly, but she only reacted to balls within her range. And her movement was sluggish, so if a line drive got past her, the batter was guaranteed a double.

... Just lose quick and go home. That works.

"Let's shut them out! Yeah!"

Haruhi was getting pumped up by herself. It goes without saying that the chest protector, shin guards, and catcher's mitt for the person on the receiving end of her pitches, Koizumi, were all borrowed.

The opposing leadoff batter bowed to the umpire before heading to the batter's box.

Haruhi threw her first pitch with an overhand motion.

Strike.

An impressive fastball with great spin, speed, and control. The pitch was right down the middle, but the force behind the ball was so intense that the bat didn't even twitch.

Naturally, I, along with the other SOS Brigade members, was not surprised. If she were suddenly named to the national soccer team, we probably still wouldn't be surprised. Anything is possible with Haruhi.

But the same couldn't be said for the opposing leadoff batter. He stood in a daze as the second pitch flew by. He finally swung on the third pitch, but unfortunately, he struck out. Her pitch

apparently had a tendency to change slightly when it reached the batter. Really vicious, just like Haruhi's personality.

The second batter, after receiving advice from the leadoff batter, gripped his bat to bunt. But after hitting two fouls, he also struck out.

I was getting worried. At this rate, the game might not be decided until the last inning. However, the meat of the order delivered. The third batter landed a solid hit on Haruhi's pitch. If you keep throwing fastballs in the strike zone, you're going to give up hits.

The ball sailed far above Nagato, who didn't move a muscle, and disappeared outside the ballpark.

Haruhi glared at the third hitter circling the infield as though she were Queen Medea, just betrayed by Jason.

In any case, we were now one run behind.

We proceeded to give up a double to the cleanup hitter, and an error by Kunikida on the fifth hitter left runners on first and second. The sixth hitter landed a Texas leaguer inside right field to bring in a second run. The seventh hitter drilled one down the third base line, but Tsuruya scooped it up effortlessly and delivered a laser to throw the batter out. Finally time to change sides.

The score at the end of the first inning was 2–0. It was surprisingly close. Except I didn't want us to put up a good fight. We needed to give up ten runs pronto so we could go home.

Our fifth, sixth, and seventh batters, my sister, Koizumi, and Kunikida, went down one after the next, and we found ourselves back out in the field for the bottom of the second before we could even catch our breath.

It appeared that the opposing team had perceived that the outfield was our weakness. They began focusing exclusively on hitting fly balls. Every time, Taniguchi and I would dash to the outfield to try to catch the ball. We were successful around 10 percent of the time and it was excessively tiring. Well, it was a small price to pay for saving Asahina from her predicament. After all, she still looked cute when she was all frightened and huddled into a ball.

And so in the end, we gave up five runs this inning. 7–0. Three runs to go. The game should be over next inning.

Top of the third inning. Our turn to go on the attack.

Tsuruya, with her long hair tied behind her back, was keeping it alive with foul balls. She appeared to be a person with good reflexes, but eventually, she popped the ball up behind her and the catcher caught it. She returned, tapping her helmet with the bat.

"That's a toughie. It was all I could manage to get the bat on the ball."

Haruhi creased her brow as she watched, seeming to be deep in thought. Nothing good ever happens when she's thinking.

"Hmm. It looks like we're going to need that."

Haruhi puckered her lips and slowly motioned to the umpire.

"Hey! Time-out!"

She then grabbed Asahina, sitting properly with a megaphone in her hand, by the neck.

"Eek!"

Haruhi disappeared behind the bench, dragging the petite, gym uniform–clad girl with her. Both of them had been carrying sports bags with them, and it soon became clear what had been inside those bags.

"W-Wait...! Suzumiya! St-Stop...it!"

I could hear bits and pieces of Asahina's adorable shrieking.

"Come on! Get undressed! We're getting changed!"

The wind carried Haruhi's booming voice to us. This again, huh?

When Asahina finally reappeared, she was wearing an exceedingly appropriate outfit for this event. A sleeveless shirt and pleated miniskirt ensemble in bright blue and white. She held yellow pompoms in both hands.

A cheerleader in every sense of the word. Where did they get an outfit like that? It's a mystery.

"Looking good there."

Kunikida commented in a carefree manner.

"Mikuru, can I take a picture?"

Tsuruya chuckled as she took out a digital camera.

I should mention that Haruhi was wearing the same outfit. She could have just worn it by herself...but I didn't feel that way. Asahina in a cheerleader outfit was, quite frankly, a ridiculously adorable sight. She looks cute no matter what she's wearing.

"It might go better with a ponytail."

Haruhi had gathered Asahina's hair together as she brushed it from behind, when she noticed my gaze and puckered her lips like a duckbill. Ponytail canceled.

"Come on. Start cheering."

"What...H-How do I do that...?"

"Like this."

Haruhi circled behind Asahina, grabbed her slender pale arms, and began waving them up and down. Like some kind of funny dance. Haruhi was loudly hissing, "Say it! Just say it!" or something in her ear.

"Eek! Everybody! Please hit the ball! Please do your best!"

Asahina screamed at the top of her lungs in a falsetto. At the very least, Taniguchi appeared to be psyched up as he recklessly swung the bat in the batter's circle. Of course, I doubt that will be enough to get a hit off the opposing pitcher.

As expected, Taniguchi returned to the bench dejected.

"Yeah, there's no way I can hit that."

That brought us back to the top of the order, and Haruhi once again stood in the batter's box.

Still wearing that cheerleader outfit.

Previously, Haruhi and Asahina had dressed up as bunny girls, which had been a spectacle rather rough on the eyes, but the impact here was much the same.

At the moment, the opposition was having difficulty deciding where to look. Asahina was wonderful in every possible way, and the same could, for the most part, be said for Haruhi, barring her personality. Like her looks or figure.

Haruhi did not overlook the fact that the pitcher, whose control suddenly went out of whack, threw a really sweet pitch. She hit it past the center fielder for another stand-up double. While some miscommunication occurred during the throw back to the infield, Haruhi slid into third base. I was wondering where the third baseman's eyes were when Haruhi slid.

And the next batter was a beautiful cheerleader whose charms surpassed those of Haruhi's. Asahina, cowering with the bat in her hands, was dizzy with embarrassment as she endured the stares of many males (including myself). Very nice.

The opposing pitcher was unable to manage anything beyond a wobbly pitch at this point, but I suppose I shouldn't have been surprised when Asahina still couldn't hit it. Even when he was throwing easy ball after easy ball.

"Eh!"

Her eyes were shut when she swung the bat, so it'd be pretty hard for her to hit anything.

Soon enough, she'd racked up two strikes. At this point, Haruhi began waving her arms around on third base. What is she doing?

"That appears to be a bunt signal," Koizumi explained calmly.

"Did we ever decide on any signals?"

"No. However, we should be able to conjecture what kind of signal Suzumiya would use in this situation. She's probably signaling for a squeeze."

"Signaling for a squeeze with two outs? Even a tenured manager would try to come up with something better than that."

"Presuming that Asahina's chances of hitting the ball are practically zero, using a squeeze play when the opposing team least expects it may possibly cause the infield to commit an error. Or perhaps she believes that even Asahina can at least manage to make contact with the ball."

"They've all figured it out, though."

Their infielders were all ready to swoop in on the ball. There was probably something wrong with Haruhi's gesturing. Everybody could tell that she was signaling for a bunt.

As expected, the squeeze play ended in failure. After all, Asahina had no idea what a squeeze was to begin with so she simply tilted her head and watched Haruhi's obvious signals with a puzzled look on her face while the third strike flew by. Three outs. Change sides.

Like a puppy resigned to being scolded by its owner, Asahina returned in low spirits and stopped when Haruhi called her over.

"Mikuru, come over here and buckle down for some pain!"

"Eh…"

Haruhi raised both hands to pinch Asahina's trembling cheeks and pulled.

"This is punishment. Punishment. Let everyone look at your funny face!"

"Pwease stop…Wit hurts…"

"Are you an idiot?"

I whacked Haruhi's head with the megaphone.

"It's your fault for giving signals that make no sense. Just steal home by yourself or something, stupid."

That was when it happened.

Ring-ring. Koizumi pulled a cell phone out of his pocket and looked at the LCD display, cocking an eyebrow.

Asahina had a startled expression on her face as she looked into the distance with one hand pressed against her left ear.

Nagato looked straight up into the sky.

Koizumi stopped me as we were dispersing across the field.

"Things have taken a bad turn."

"I really don't want to hear it, but go ahead."

"Closed space has just appeared. On a scale never before witnessed. It appears to be expanding at an alarming rate."

Closed space.

The gray world I was already familiar with. As if I could ever forget. Getting stuck in that gloomy space left me traumatized for life.

Koizumi continued to smile.

"Allow me to explain. Closed space is an unconscious way for Suzumiya to release stress. And Suzumiya happens to be in a foul mood at the moment. Therefore, closed space has appeared, and as long as Suzumiya retains her foul mood, it will continue

to expand, and the Celestials you are well acquainted with will continue to rampage. There you have it."

"...So you're saying that Haruhi's got her panties in a bunch because we're losing a baseball game? And it's so bad that she's creating that stupid space?"

"So it would appear."

"Is she a child?!"

Koizumi didn't reply. He simply chuckled. I sighed.

"She's so full of it."

Koizumi gave me a look.

"You're still saying things like that at this point? And you sound as though it doesn't concern you. The ordeal before us is largely related to you. We used a lottery to determine the batting order, correct?"

"A ladder lottery, yeah. What about it?"

"And consequently, you became cleanup."

"I'm not particularly happy about that."

"It doesn't matter to Suzumiya whether you feel happy or under pressure. The issue here is the fact that you drew cleanup."

"Explain in a way I can understand."

"It is very simple. You became the cleanup batter because Suzumiya desired it. This wasn't a coincidence. Suzumiya wished for you to play a big role as the cleanup batter. And then she was disappointed by your dismal performance."

"So sorry about that."

"Yes, I am also troubled by the current situation. At this rate, Suzumiya's mood will only continue to worsen and closed space will continue to expand."

"...So, what am I supposed to do about it?"

"Hit the ball. A long hit if possible. A home run would be terrific. Especially if it were a huge one. How about trying to bounce one off the scoreboard?"

"Don't be ridiculous. I've only ever hit home runs in video

31

games. And there's no way I'm going to hit a ball that curves like that."

"All of the concerned parties sincerely wish that you can do something about this ordeal."

"Wishing isn't going to help when I'm not a genie or a monkey's paw."

"Let us do everything possible to prevent the game from being called this inning. If we allow the game to end now, it will mean the end of the world. We must do all we can to hold them to two runs."

Koizumi didn't look very worried, considering the gravity of his words.

Bottom of the third. Haruhi went to the pitcher's mound without changing clothes. Asahina was also wearing the cheerleader outfit as she stood in right field.

Haruhi had no qualms about exposing her bare limbs as she went into the same windup motion she used regardless of whether or not any runners were on base.

The first batter hit a line drive that happened to be on a direct course for Nagato, which led to an out. But she didn't even turn her head to look at the second batter's deep fly that landed between left and center for a triple. Haruhi's red-hot pitches were as strong as ever, but if you keep throwing fastballs, you're bound to give up hits. No wonder these guys are a lock for the championship. Following that, two hits and a fielder's choice by Kunikida led to two more runs. Our backs were against the wall at this point. And there were runners on first and second. The game would be called after another run. And who knows what would happen to the world then.

Clang. The white ball shot into the air. Headed toward right field. Asahina was all flustered in the vicinity of where the ball would land. No time to think. I sprinted with all my might to the right side of the field for the umpteenth time. Make it in time!

I dove. And caught the ball. The ball sat in the tip of my glove.

"There!"

I then threw the ball as hard as I could to Taniguchi, who had moved over to cover second. The runner had been expecting extra bases on that hit since he didn't even bother tagging up before he started running. Taniguchi stepped on the base with the ball in his glove. Out. Double play.

We somehow pulled it off. Man, I'm exhausted.

"Nice play!"

I basked in Asahina's admiring gaze and flashed a victory sign as Taniguchi, Kunikida, my sister, and Tsuruya all walked by and patted my head with their gloves. I glanced at Haruhi to find her glaring at the scoreboard (which was basically a portable whiteboard) with a troubled look on her face.

As I sat down on the bench with a towel over my head, Koizumi walked over.

"Picking up where we left off..."

I really don't want to hear it.

"There actually is a way to remedy the current situation. During the previous incident, when you and Suzumiya were in the other world, how did you make it back?"

Seriously, don't remind me of that.

"If we use that method again, it may get us out of the current crisis."

"I refuse."

Koizumi chuckled. "You're really starting to piss me off."

"I thought you would say that. How does this sound then? We just have to win the game. I just had an excellent idea. I'm sure it will go well. After all, her interests should coincide with ours."

And with a grin on his face, Koizumi walked off toward the white circle where Nagato was standing still. The only part of her that showed any sign of movement was her short hair swaying in the breeze as Koizumi appeared to whisper something in her ear. Unexpectedly, Nagato turned her head to look at me with emotionless eyes.

Did she just nod her head? Her head bobbed like the head of a puppet whose strings had just been cut, before she trudged off to the batter's box.

I glanced left to find Asahina staring at Nagato this time.

"Nagato's finally…"

Her face paled as she voiced those curious words.

"Is something up with her?"

"Nagato appears to be reciting an incantation."

"Incantation? What's that?"

"Um…That's classified."

Asahina bowed her head apologetically. It's fine, really. I can't do anything about it if it's classified. Huh, I guess something unimaginable is about to happen again.

I could recall a thing or two regarding Nagato's incantations.

One unusually hot evening back in May. If Nagato hadn't barged into the classroom that day, I would certainly be resting in a grave somewhere. Nagato had muttered some kind of incantation at a ridiculous speed to repel the attacker who had tried to kill me. Oh, right. Nagato was still wearing glasses back then.

I wonder what she's going to do this time.

I found out soon enough.

One swing of the bat. Home run.

Nagato barely used any strength when she swung the bat yet she connected with the center of the pitcher's fastball and launched it into the sky before it disappeared beyond the fence.

I turned to look at my teammates. Koizumi had an elegant smile on his face as he nodded in my direction. Asahina's face looked a bit stiff but she didn't seem to be surprised. My sister and Tsuruya were innocently going, "That was awesome!" in admiration.

However, everybody else was simply dumbfounded. Including the members of the opposing team.

Haruhi skipped over to home plate to tap the helmet of Nagato, who had indifferently finished her lap around the bases.

"That was incredible! Where are you hiding that strength?"

She took Nagato's arms and bent them back and forth. Nagato stood still with a blank look on her face and let Haruhi have her way.

Eventually, Nagato walked over to the bench and handed me the bat.

"Here."

She pointed at the worn metal bat.

"This has been modified with a boost in attribute data," she said.

"What's that mean?" I asked. Nagato stared at me for a while.

"Homing mode."

And with that, she trotted back to the bench and sat down on the end before burying herself in a thick book she picked up from below.

The score was now 9–1 in the top of the fourth. It appeared that this would be the last inning.

It appeared that their pitcher hadn't entirely recovered from his shock, but his pitches were still more than fast enough as far as I was concerned.

And then I found out what Nagato had meant.

"Whoa!"

The bat moved on its own. Dragging my arms and shoulders with it. *Clang.*

I thought that I'd barely hit the ball, but it went flying over the stands as though carried by the wind past the grass and into the next field. Home run. Jaws dropped.

I see. Homing mode, is it...

I tossed aside the bat, which had apparently obtained the ability to automatically go after balls and hit them twice as far as normally possible, and began jogging around the bases.

Once I reached second base, I looked up and my eyes met Haruhi's as she waved her arms up and down, but she quickly looked away. You could just celebrate the way my sister and Tsuruya are. As far as I could tell, Taniguchi and Kunikida were astonished while Asahina, Koizumi, and Nagato were silent, and the nine members of the opposing team had looks of bewilderment on their faces.

I was feeling pretty guilty, but the opposing team wasn't done being astonished.

My sister tottered over to the batter's box next with the batter's helmet hiding over half of her face since it was too big. I'm surprised she could even walk straight. The secret weapon I'd prepared to ensure our defeat took a full swing at the first pitch and sent it flying over the fence. In other words, what most people call a home run.

There's a limit to how ridiculous you can be. A little girl in fifth grade just sent an eighty mph (estimate) pitch thrown by a college student all the way to the main stands. It's hard to believe this is happening in reality.

"Amazing!"

Haruhi didn't doubt reality for a second. She greeted my sister, who had quickly circled the bases, and swung her around, all smiles.

"What wonderful talent! You have a bright future ahead of you! You could definitely make it in the majors!"

My sister squealed cheerfully as Haruhi swung her around.

This is just…Whatever, the score's 9–3 now.

I was sitting on the bench and holding my head.

Our home run offensive was still under way. The score was now 9–7. Seven straight home runs in one inning. I'm assuming that we set a tournament record.

Taniguchi returned after a big hit.

"I've decided to join the baseball team. I could make it to the nationals with my batting sense. After all, it felt like the bat was hitting the ball by itself!"

Kunikida stood next to him sounding overly optimistic.

"Yeah, no kidding."

As their mind-numbing conversation continued, Tsuruya was slapping Asahina, who looked unusually stiff, on the shoulder and laughing loudly. It's a good thing they're all so simple.

"You and me! Man-to-man!" Haruhi said as she held the bat. Isn't the pitcher the one who's supposed to say that?

The metallic clang I was already sick of hearing rang again and the ball bounced off the scoreboard.

That made the score 9–8. During this period, the opposing team had gone through three pitchers. They probably didn't want my sympathy, but they got it anyway. Poor guys.

We completed a rotation as Asahina, Nagato, and I hit consecutive home runs and we finally took the lead 11–9. Eleven consecutive home runs. I was starting to feel like this was getting pretty dangerous. Since I had a feeling that the members of the opposing team were looking at our bat instead of our players. They probably figured it was some kind of magic bat. I guess they weren't exactly wrong.

Before I handed the bat to the next person up, my sister, I brought Nagato away from the end of the bench where she'd been reading.

"That's enough," I said as Nagato's expressionless black eyes actually blinked multiple times in succession as opposed to her customary one blink every ten seconds or so.

"I see," she responded.

She placed her thin fingers on the handle of the bat I was carrying and recited something really fast. I couldn't make out what she said, but I doubt I would have understood it if I had, so it didn't really matter.

Nagato then removed her fingers, returned to the bench, and picked her book up again without saying a word.

Good grief.

My sister, Koizumi, and Kunikida struck out so fast you had to wonder if their previous hits had been some kind of fluke. In fact, it'd been plain cheating.

I'd forgotten, but this match had a time limit. In the first round, ninety minutes was the limit. The organizers had done this so they could get through all the necessary matches today. Therefore, the next inning would be dropped. If we lasted through the bottom of the fourth, we would win.

Is it really okay for us to win?

"We cannot afford the alternative," said Koizumi.

"I have received word from my colleagues. Thanks to our efforts, the expansion of closed space has been checked. However, the Celestials remain so we still have to deal with those. But it would be a great help if no more of them show up."

But if they make a comeback now, it'll be a walk-off loss. There's no need to think about how bad Haruhi's mood will be then.

"And so I have an idea concerning that."

Koizumi smiled to reveal teeth so white I wanted to tell him to go do a toothbrush commercial. He whispered his idea to me.

"Seriously?"

"I am very serious. This is our only remaining option if we wish to make it through this inning while giving up a minimal number of runs."

Once again, good grief.

We informed the umpire of a change in positions.

Nagato would take over as catcher for Koizumi. Koizumi would move to center field. And I was switching positions with Haruhi to stand on the mound.

Haruhi was grumbling when Koizumi first informed her about the pitching change, but then she made a face once she found out I was the relief pitcher.

"...Well, okay, I guess. But if you give up a hit, you have to buy everyone lunch!"

And with that, she retreated to second base.

Nagato was just standing there like she was spaced out while Koizumi and I put the chest protector and facemask and whatever on her. You sure about letting such a gloomy girl be catcher?

Nagato trudged to her spot behind home plate and squatted down.

Okay, time for the match to restart. There wasn't much time left, so I didn't get a chance to warm up. I have to throw the first pitch of my life on the fly.

In any case, I gave it a throw.

Whuff.

The ball somehow managed to land in Nagato's glove. Ball.

"Take this seriously!"

That was Haruhi shouting back there. I'm always dead serious, man. I tried to sidearm it this time.

The second pitch. I was hoping that the batter might be fooled a little, but no such luck. His bat rushed straight for my weak pitch. Damn, I basically fed that one to him!

Smack.

"Strike!"

The umpire yelled loudly. He swung and missed so that would be a strike. However, the batter was looking at Nagato's hand with an incredulous expression on his face.

I understood how he felt. How else would he react? Anybody would be in disbelief after watching my weak ball abruptly drop thirty centimeters right when it was on the verge of making contact with the bat.

"..."

Nagato remained squatting as she snapped her wrist to return the ball to me. After catching her floater, I wound up to pitch again.

Every time I threw the ball, it turned into some kind of half-assed fastball. And my third pitch was way off the mark—or it would have been if it hadn't changed course after a few meters, curving in a way that obviously ignored stuff like inertia and gravity and aerodynamics. It even managed to accelerate before it landed in the catcher's mitt. *Smack.* That was a good sound. Nagato's small body shook a bit.

The batter's eyes were as wide as saucers. The umpire was also speechless. After a while, he finally opened his mouth.

"...Strike two!"

He didn't sound very confident. This is getting annoying so I'll just get it over with.

I was just randomly throwing the ball at this point. Not even trying to aim or anything. Not using much strength to throw the ball either. Nonetheless, every ball I threw would go inside the strike zone if the batter didn't swing, and curve if he did.

The secret lay in whatever Nagato was mumbling every time I threw the ball. And it was so secret that I had no idea how it worked either. It was probably some sort of data manipulation like how she'd previously saved my life and reconstructed the classroom or whatever she did to the bat earlier.

As a result, this was like pitching to an electric fan. Without a doubt, Yuki Nagato was the MVP for the day.

In no time, the opposing team had racked up two outs and the last batter was at a 2–0 count. Should it really be this easy for me to close the game? Sorry, Kamigahara Pirates.

I turned to the batter, whose face was pale at this point, and threw a normal pitch without exerting any effort.

The ball changed course toward the strike zone. The batter swung with all his might. The ball changed course again toward the outside corner. The bat swung around so hard you could see an afterimage. Strikeout. Whew, it was finally over…except it wasn't.

"!"

The ball spun toward the backstop. It appeared that she'd gone overboard on the curve. The ball grazed Nagato's catcher's mitt and the Mystery Ball (my name for it) sank like a forkball before bouncing off a corner of home plate and rolling off.

It was a wild pitch.

Given this last chance, the batter dashed off. However, Nagato remained frozen in her catcher's stance, squatting in silence with her facemask still on.

"Nagato! Pick up the ball and throw it!"

Nagato looked up blankly in response to my instructions before slowly standing up and chasing the loose ball. At an excruciatingly slow pace. The batter had already touched first base and was attempting to make it to second.

"Hurry!"

Haruhi was standing on second base and waving her glove around.

Nagato finally caught up to the ball and picked it up, staring at it as though it were a sea turtle egg. She then turned to me.

"Second!"

I pointed straight behind me. Haruhi was standing there shouting at the top of her lungs. Nagato nodded her head about a millimeter—

Whoosh. A white laser beam passed the side of my head. It took a few strands of my hair with it. I didn't realize the laser was Nagato throwing the ball using only her wrist until I saw the ball knock Haruhi's glove off her hand and all the way into center field.

Haruhi was staring at her previously gloved hand while the runner had apparently fallen down right in front of second base in terror.

Koizumi, the center fielder, picked up the glove and withdrew the ball before walking over to the batter-runner with his universal beaming smile on his face as he bent down to tag him out. Then he apologized.

"I'm terribly sorry. We happen to be a slightly unreasonable group."

As I wondered if he was including me in that unreasonable group, I released a deep sigh.

Game over.

The members of the Kamigahara Pirates were weeping. I didn't really get it, though. Were they going to be punished by alumni later? Or were they just frustrated by the fact that they lost to a team of high school amateurs that had more females than males and included a girl in grade school. Probably both.

On the other hand, Haruhi, who obviously didn't care about the grief the losers were feeling, was in high spirits. She had a smile on her face much like the one she had back on that day when she came up with the idea of creating the SOS Brigade.

"Let's win this tournament and enter the national tournament this summer! Dominating the entire country isn't just a dream!"

She was shouting stuff like that in a serious tone. Taniguchi was the only one who looked interested, though. I merely wished that she would give it a break already, and I'm pretty sure the High School Baseball Federation felt the same way.

"Excellent work."

Koizumi had come over next to me while I wasn't paying attention.

"By the way, what do we do now? Shall we continue into the second round?"

I shook my head.

"So basically, Haruhi will be in a bad mood if we lose, right? Which would mean we have to keep winning. That would require more of Nagato's bogus magic. No matter how you look at it, it's pretty obvious that there's going to be trouble if we keep ignoring the laws of physics. Let's forfeit."

"That sounds best. The truth is that I need to go help my colleagues soon. To eliminate closed space. It appears that they need more people to deal with the Celestials."

"Say hello to your people for me. To those blue guys too."

"I shall do that. In any case, this incident has taught us that it is a bad idea to allow Suzumiya to be bored. We should take that into consideration during future endeavors."

After telling me to take care of the rest, Koizumi headed off

toward the administrative tent to inform them that we wouldn't
be advancing to the second round.

He left me with the harder job. Guess I don't really have a choice.

I walked over to where Haruhi was forcing Asahina to dance
the can-can with her and poked her in the back.

"What? You want to dance with us?"

"We need to talk."

I took Haruhi outside the field. She became unexpectedly quiet.

"Look over there."

I motioned toward the bench where the Kamigahara Pirates
were sobbing.

"Don't you feel bad for them?"

"Why?"

"They've probably undergone intensive training for this day. The
opportunity to become the champion for four years running was
on the line so they were probably under a lot of pressure."

"So?"

"They probably have a few benchwarmers who didn't even get a
chance to play, that are holding back their tears. Yeah, like that
guy with the crew cut behind the net. You really have to feel bad
for him, right? He's never going to get a chance to play."

"What's your point?"

"Let's forfeit."

I just said it flat out.

"You've had your fun, right? I've had enough to share with anyone
who asks. I'd rather just go grab lunch and talk about stupid stuff.
To be honest, my arms and legs are completely worn out."

That was the truth. After all that running between the infield
and outfield, I was physically exhausted. Mentally too.

Haruhi then made her favorite face, the one that resembled a
sulking pelican, as she glared up at me. I was starting to get worried when she finally spoke up.

"You're okay with that?"

"I sure am. Asahina, Koizumi, and even Nagato probably feel the same way. My sister's been over there practicing her swinging for a while now, but if you give her some candy, she'll drop the bat."

"Hmm."

Haruhi alternated looks between me and the field as she thought it over. Or maybe she was just pretending to think it over. She grinned.

"I guess that's fine then. I'm pretty hungry anyway. Let's go have lunch. I was thinking, baseball sure is a simple sport. I didn't expect to win so easily."

Really.

I kept my mouth shut and shrugged.

When I told the captain of the opposing team that we were letting them advance to the second round in our place, he began thanking me profusely while weeping. That just made me feel even guiltier. After all, we basically stole that win by using some ridiculous methods of cheating.

I had immediately turned to leave when the captain told me to hold on and whispered in my ear.

"By the way, how much do you want for the bat you guys were using?"

And so, at the moment, our group, excluding Koizumi, was occupying the corner of a family restaurant and chowing down.

My sister had grown attached to Haruhi and Asahina and sat between two of them, stabbing at her hamburger steak with a

knife in a dangerous fashion. Taniguchi was holding a serious discussion with Kunikida about how he was going to join the baseball team. Yeah, he can do whatever he wants. Tsuruya's attention was now focused on Nagato. "So you're Yuki Nagato? I've heard a lot about you from Mikuru." Her random chatter was ignored by her reticent underclassman, who silently munched away at her BLT sandwich.

Everybody had ordered way more than necessary, but that was expected. Since I was paying for everybody.

Haruhi had announced that little tidbit as though it were some kind of brilliant idea. I have no idea how Haruhi came up with it. Nobody has ever been able to trace her pattern of thought, so I wasn't exactly surprised. I didn't bother protesting because it would have been too much of a pain. In fact, I was in a pretty good mood.

Because I'd managed to get my hands on some unexpected extra cash.

Here's to the success of the Kamigahara Pirates.

The following happened a few days later.

After school one day, we were in our room in the clubhouse, living another normal day as usual.

I was playing Othello with Koizumi as I drank tea made by Asahina in her maid outfit. Nagato sat next to us reading a philosophy book she'd borrowed from the library that looked like a thick dictionary. By the way, Asahina was dressed according to my request today. It's definitely better to be served by a maid than by a nurse. And Asahina stood carrying a tray as she intently watched our match.

This was the usual scene in this room as of late.

And this peaceful time, as tranquil as the grand Yellow River, was always ruined by Haruhi Suzumiya.

"Sorry I'm late!"

Haruhi apologized for no reason as she jumped in like a cold winter draft.

Her entire face was lit up by a smile, which gave me the creeps. Whenever she smiles like that, something's bound to happen that will leave me exhausted. We live in a funny world.

As expected, Haruhi had something stupid to say.

"Which one do you want?"

I placed a black piece on the board and flipped over two of Koizumi's white pieces.

"Which what?"

"This."

Haruhi held out two sheets of paper. I reluctantly took them.

More flyers again. I looked them over. One was for a soccer tournament. The other was for a football tournament. I'm seriously going to curse whoever it is that prints these things out.

"I was actually planning on doing one of these two instead of baseball. But the baseball tournament just happened to be earlier. So, Kyon, which one do you want?"

I succumbed to my feelings of gloom and looked around the club room. Koizumi smiled wryly as he flicked at his pieces. Asahina was shaking her head with tears in her eyes. Nagato remained buried in her books with her fingers being the only part of her body showing any sign of movement.

"So how many people do you need for soccer and football? Will the roster from last time suffice?"

As I watched the glowing smile on Haruhi's face, I tried to figure out which one would require fewer people.

BAMBOO LEAF RHAPSODY

Come to think of it, May had been a pretty hot month, temperature-wise, but here we were in July, and it was even hotter. Plus, the humidity was rising at such a ridiculous rate that my discomfort index was off the charts. The cheap-looking buildings that made up our high school were completely free of any fancy comforts such as air conditioners. The interior of the 1-5 classroom felt like a burning waiting room to hell, which made you wonder if the person who designed this place understood what amenities were.

On top of that, we were in the first week of July, with finals around the corner, so my happy feelings had wandered off to somewhere in the vicinity of Brazil and wouldn't be returning anytime soon.

Midterms had been quite a disaster, and at this rate, I seriously doubted I'd get a decent grade on my finals. And there was no denying that the problem was due to too much time spent on SOS Brigade activities and not enough time devoted to studying. Not that I chose to spend my time on that crap, but a rule had been established in spring that every time Haruhi said something, I had to go from place to place for no real reason at all, and this was now my part of normal lifestyle. I really hated how I was growing accustomed to this practice.

We were sitting in the classroom during a break with sunlight streaming in from the west. The girl sitting behind me poked me in the back with her pencil.

"Do you know what day it is?"

Haruhi Suzumiya said this with a look on her face like she was a grade schooler on Christmas Eve. When she starts showing this much emotion on her face, it's a signal that she's up to no good. I spent three seconds pretending to think.

"Your birthday?"

"No."

"Asahina's birthday."

"No!"

"Koizumi's or Nagato's birthday."

"I don't even know when those are."

"Incidentally, my birthday is—"

"I don't care. You have no idea what an important day it is, do you?"

You can say whatever you want, but as far as I'm concerned, it's just a really hot weekday.

"Tell me what month and what day it is."

"July seventh…This seems like a stretch, but don't tell me you're talking about Tanabata."

"Of course I am. It's Tanabata, you know. Every Japanese person is supposed to remember Tanabata."

First of all, that actually began as a Chinese tradition. And Tanabata, the Star Festival, is supposed to be next month if you go by the Chinese calendar.

Haruhi waved her pencil in front of my face.

"Everything this side of the Red Sea is considered Asia."

That's an odd way to describe geography.

"We're in the same block for the World Cup preliminaries, right? And there isn't much of a difference between July and August. It's still summer."

Oh, really.

"Whatever. We have to do a proper job of celebrating Tanabata. I always throw myself into these kinds of events."

I'm pretty sure there are better things for you to throw yourself into. And more importantly, why is it necessary for you to tell me this? I could care less about what you want to do.

"It's more fun if everyone participates. Starting this year, all the brigade members will get together for a big party on Tanabata."

"Don't decide that on your own."

I was watching a needlessly triumphant look on Haruhi's face as I protested, which left me feeling that it was stupid to bother to try to object.

And once class was over for the day, Haruhi flew out of the classroom the second the bell rang.

"I'll be waiting in the club room! You're not allowed to go home!" she said in parting.

I didn't need her to tell me to go to the club room. After all, there happens to be a person I try to meet at least once a day. The only such person.

The other brigade members had already assembled in the SOS Brigade's hideout, the literary club room on the second floor of the clubhouse, a place where we would be considered parasites rather than tenants.

"Ah, hello."

That greeting came from Mikuru Asahina, who had a bright smile on her face. She's the source of my peace. An SOS Brigade without her would be as meaningless as curry rice without the curry.

Since it was July, Asahina had switched to a summer version of her maid outfit. Who knew where Haruhi had brought the costume from, but upon receiving it, Asahina had sincerely thanked her by saying, "Ah, thank you very much." She was serving as the SOS Brigade's maid again today, earnestly making tea for me. As I drank the tea, I looked across the room.

"Hello, how are you doing?"

Itsuki Koizumi nodded to me from his seat in front of a chessboard at the long table as he moved pieces around with one hand and held a book of chess problems in the other.

"I've been going insane ever since I started high school."

Last week, Koizumi had brought the board after saying something about trying out chess since he was getting tired of Othello. Unfortunately, I didn't know the rules, and neither did any of the other people here so he was left playing chess by his lonesome, which I supposed was an indication that he had nothing to worry about regarding the upcoming exams.

"I wouldn't say that I have nothing to worry about. This is merely a means of exercising my brain while taking a break from studying. Every problem solved improves the blood circulation in my brain. Would you care to join me?"

No thanks. I don't feel like doing any more thinking than I have to. Plus, I have a feeling that if I learn any of this weird stuff, it'll boot the English vocabulary words I have to remember out of my memory.

"That's unfortunate. Shall I bring LIFE or Battleship next time? Yes, it would be a good idea to bring something that everyone could play. What would you recommend?"

Anything works. Though at the same time, nothing would really be acceptable. This is the SOS Brigade, not a board game club. Incidentally, the objective of the SOS Brigade's activities remains a mystery to me, so I still have no idea what this enigmatic brigade is supposed to do. Not that I really want to know, and I'm probably safer off not knowing. Which is why I don't feel like doing anything. My logic is perfect.

Koizumi shrugged and returned to his book of problems. He took a black knight and moved it to a new position.

Next to Koizumi was Yuki Nagato, buried in a book and showing less emotion than an animatronics puppet in some B movie. It appeared that the reticent and curt pseudo-alien had finally developed a taste for reading original texts instead of their translated versions. The book she was currently reading looked like some kind of ancient and heavy spell book with a title scribbled in some kind of Fraktur script I couldn't decipher. I'm pretty sure it was written in ancient Etruscan or something. Nagato would probably have no problem reading a Linear A inscription on a stone tablet.

I pulled back the metal chair and took a seat. Asahina immediately set a cup down in front of me. It's really a bad idea to drink hot tea in this sweltering weather—except that I most definitely was not harboring such a wrongful thought. I simply sipped my tea with a heartfelt sense of gratitude. Yep, it's hot and sweltering.

An electric fan that Haruhi had brought in from who knows where was whirring away in the corner of the room, but it was about as effective as pouring boiling water onto hot stone. She should have just stolen an air conditioner from the faculty office.

I looked up from my English textbook with its pages flipping in the breeze, and leaned back into the metal chair to stretch.

It wasn't like I was going to study when I got home, so I figured I might as well try to get some studying done after school in the club room, but as I discovered, a change in location isn't going to make you want to do something you don't want to do. It's bad for both the body and the mind to do something you don't want to do.

In other words, you'll live a healthier life if you don't do what you don't want to do. Okay, I quit. I spun my pencil, shut the textbook, and decided to watch my sedative. I was referring to the sedative for soothing my pessimistic soul, by which I mean the maid sitting across the table and working on her math problem set.

She stared earnestly at her problem set as she periodically scribbled in her notebook before becoming deep in thought with a listless look on her face until she jumped as though a lightbulb had gone off in her head and her pencil raced across the paper. And naturally, the girl repeating this cycle was none other than Mikuru Asahina.

The mere sight of her is enough to calm me down. I was feeling so amiable that I would have been willing to donate more than just a few coins to the bell ringers on the streets. Asahina was so focused on studying math that she didn't even notice me watching her. Every one of her movements was enough to make me smile. In fact, I had a big grin plastered on my face. I felt like I was watching a baby seal.

Our eyes met.

"Ah. Wh-What is it? Did I do something strange?"

Asahina looked herself over in a fluster. That was quite a fine sight and I was about to deliver some form of angel metaphor when…

"Hey, hey!"

The door flew open and the rude girl made her rude entrance.

"Sorriez. Didn't mean to be late."

No need to apologize. Nobody was waiting for you.

Haruhi showed up speaking in a boisterous voice with a chunky stalk of bamboo over her shoulder. It was a fresh one, thick with deep green bamboo leaves.

"Why did you bring that here? Are you planning on making a safe box or something?"

Haruhi puffed up in response.

"To hang wish cards on, obviously."

Why? For what reason?

"No real reason. I just suddenly felt like doing it and it's been a while. Plus we get to hang up our wishes. Since today is Tanabata after all."

...As always, her actions truly had no meaning.

"Where'd you get that from?"

"The thicket behind our school."

Pretty sure that's private property. Damn bamboo thief.

"Who cares, really? The roots are still under the earth so it doesn't matter if one stalk on the surface is missing. Though it might be considered a crime if I stole a bamboo shoot. Anyway, I'm all itchy after being bitten by mosquitoes. Mikuru, could you apply some ointment to my back?"

"Ah...yes! At once!"

Asahina quickly ran over with the first aid kit in her hands. She looked like a nurse in training as she took out the tube of ointment and stuck her hand under the hem of Haruhi's sailor uniform to reach her back. Haruhi continued talking as she bent forward.

"A little more to the right...That's too far right. Yeah, that's the spot."

Haruhi closed her eyes like a kitten being scratched on its chin, but once the bamboo was placed next to the window, she stood on top of the brigade chief's desk before pulling a number of paper cards out of nowhere. She smiled cheerfully.

"Come on, write down your wishes."

Nagato abruptly looked up. Koizumi had a mocking smile on his face. Asahina's eyes were as wide as saucers. This came out of nowhere, and now she's pulling leaves off the bamboo. Haruhi hopped off the desk with a flip of her skirt.

"But there are conditions."

"What?"

"Kyon, do you know who grants wishes on Tanabata?"

"Orihime and Hikoboshi, right?"

"Correct, ten points. Then, do you know what stars Orihime and Hikoboshi refer to?"

"No clue."

"Vega and Altair, I believe."

Koizumi promptly answered.

"Exactly! Eighty-five points! Those are the exact stars I was referring to! In other words, we should hang the wish cards facing those stars. Got it?"

"What are you trying to say? And what would the remaining fifteen points cover?"

"Ahem," was the arrogant response from Haruhi.

"Allow me to explain. First of all, it is impossible to travel faster than the speed of light. That fact is based on the special theory of relativity."

What's with the lecture out of nowhere? Haruhi reached into her skirt pocket, pulled out a crumpled up sheet of notepaper, and glanced at her notes.

"By the way, the distances from Earth to Vega and Altair are twenty-five light-years and sixteen light-years respectively. Which means that any data sent from Earth will naturally take twenty-five years or sixteen years to reach its respective star, right?"

So what? And you actually bothered to research this stuff?

"So it means that it'll take a fair amount of time before either god can read your wish. So our wishes won't be granted for a while. Make sure you write down whatever you want to happen in your future twenty-five years from now or sixteen years from now! If you put down something like, 'I want a cool boyfriend by next Christmas!' it won't be granted in time!"

Haruhi stated this emphatically as she waved her arms around.

"Hey, hold on a second. If it takes around twenty-five years to make the trip there, shouldn't it take just as long to return? So wouldn't our wishes be fulfilled in fifty years or thirty-two years?"

"We're talking about gods here. They'll work that out somehow. This only happens once a year, like a fifty percent summer sale."

And she ignores relativity when it suits her purpose.

"Okay, everyone. You all understand what's going on, right? We're doing two different kinds of wish cards. One set goes to Vega and the other goes to Altair. So, write down whatever wishes you want to be granted in twenty-five years or sixteen years."

An unreasonable statement. First of all, you have to be pretty shameless to ask for two kinds of wishes. Besides, how can I make any wishes when I have no idea what I'll be doing in twenty-five years or sixteen years? The only thing I can think of would be that Social Security and Wall Street haven't gone belly-up and are still functioning properly. Pretty sure that both Orihime and Hikoboshi would be annoyed by such wishes. They only get to meet each other once a year so they probably feel that the government should deal with those issues themselves. At least, that's how I'd feel.

Still, she always comes up with these pointless ideas. Does she have a white hole inside her head or something? I wonder what universe her common sense is from.

"You can't say that for sure."

Koizumi sounded like he was taking Haruhi's side. Except he spoke in a soft voice that could only be heard by me.

"Suzumiya's actions may be eccentric, but nevertheless, she has a strong grasp on her common sense."

Koizumi flashed his usual cheerful smile at me.

"If her pattern of thought were abnormal, this world would not be as stable as it is. The world would become a bizarre place governed by odd principles."

"How can you tell?" I asked.

"Suzumiya wishes for the world to become a stranger place.

And she happens to possess the power to reconstruct this world. You should be well aware of this."

I sure am. Though I still have my doubts.

"However, the world has yet to lose its reason. Which means she is putting common sense before her personal desires."

"This is a rather childish example," Koizumi said by way of introducing his next little spiel.

"Assume, for instance, that she wanted Santa Claus to exist. However, common sense dictates that Santa could not possibly exist. It would be impossible for someone to sneak into highly secured houses late at night without being spotted by anyone, at least in modern Japan. And how does Saint Nicholas know what every single child wants? He couldn't possibly have time to visit the home of every single good child in the world in one night. It's physically impossible."

Any person who seriously thinks about this stuff has issues.

"You are absolutely right. Which is why Santa Claus does not exist."

I was only arguing against him because I didn't like how he was defending Haruhi, but I just voiced another question.

"If that's the case, shouldn't aliens, time travelers, and espers not exist the way Santa doesn't? So why are you here?"

"That is why Suzumiya is growing frustrated with her own common sense. Her common sense denies her desire for a world where supernatural phenomena frequently occur."

So in the end, her common sense lost?

"I'm sure that some unrepressed desires called Asahina, Nagato, and myself to this place and granted me mysterious powers. Though I have no idea as to why you are here."

And let's keep it that way. At the very least, I, unlike you, am confident in the fact that I am a normal human being.

58

Though I still don't know if I should be happy about that or not.

"Over there! No whispering. I'm talking about something serious here."

I suppose that the sight of Koizumi and me whispering had been an eyesore. Haruhi was yelling at us with her eyes narrowed so we had no choice but to take the cards and pencils she handed to us and return to our seats.

Haruhi was humming as her pen raced across her card. Nagato just stood there staring at hers. Asahina had a puzzled look on her face as though she were trying to solve the Königsberg bridge problem. Koizumi simply said, "What a quandary," in a carefree tone and tilted his head. There's no reason for the three of them to think so hard about it. Just have to make something up.

...Don't tell me that they expect what we write down to actually become reality.

I spun my pencil around as I looked to the side. The stalk of bamboo that had been chopped off by Haruhi sat poking through the open window with its leaves sticking every which way. An occasional passing breeze would set them rustling and cool the room down.

"Hey, did you finish writing yours?"

I turned in response to Haruhi's voice. The cards on the table in front of her read as follows:

I WISH FOR THE WORLD TO REVOLVE AROUND ME

I WISH FOR THE EARTH TO ROTATE IN THE OTHER DIRECTION

She almost sounded like some kind of obnoxious little kid. It wouldn't be a problem if she meant for it to be a joke, but the look on her face as she hung the wish cards on the bamboo leaf was dead serious.

Asahina had written hers with adorable and neat handwriting.

I WISH TO GET BETTER AT SEWING

I WISH TO GET BETTER AT COOKING

What a sweet thing to ask for. Asahina clasped her hands together and closed her eyes to pray in front of the wish cards. I think she's confused about how this works.

Nagato's cards were pretty bland. They just had the dreary words HARMONY and REFORM written in a printed-style handwriting.

As for Koizumi, he was pretty much on the same level as Nagato with the phrases THE WORLD AT PEACE and THE PEACE AND PROSPERITY OF MY FAMILY written in surprisingly messy handwriting.

And me? My wishes were simple. After all, they wouldn't come true for another twenty-five years or sixteen years. I'd be a pretty old man by that point so I'm sure that I would wish for the following:

FORK OVER MONEY

GIVE ME A TWO-STORY HOUSE WITH A LAWN

"You're such a Philistine."

Haruhi commented in a tone of disgust as she looked at the wish cards I had hung up. She's the last person who should be acting disgusted with someone. My wishes are far more productive than wishing for the world to rotate the other way.

"Well, whatever. Everybody, make sure you remember what you wrote down. The first point comes in sixteen years. We'll compete to see whose wish Hikoboshi grants first!"

"Ah…yes. Yes."

I glanced over at Asahina nodding earnestly as I sat down in my original metal chair. I turned to find that Nagato had gone back to reading her book.

Haruhi secured the long stalk of bamboo through the window before pulling a chair over next to the it and plopping down. She propped her elbow on the windowsill and stared up at the sky. The fact that she looked awfully gloomy from the side made me feel uneasy. She has severe mood swing issues. She was just shouting and yelling a second ago.

I opened my textbook in an attempt to resume my studying and tried to memorize the different types of relative pronouns.

"...Sixteen years, huh. That's a long time," I heard Haruhi murmuring behind me.

While Nagato continued to read Western books in silence, Koizumi returned to playing chess by himself, and I memorized whole chunks of English translation, Haruhi spent the entire time sitting next to the window and looking up at the sky. I can't deny that she looks good if she keeps her mouth shut and stays still. I was wondering if she'd decided to follow Nagato's brooding behavior, but a dejected Haruhi was creepy in its own right. Because it's a sure sign that she's thinking about something that will cause trouble for the rest of us.

Still, Haruhi seemed to be in particularly low spirits today. She would look up at the sky and sigh deeply. She's getting creepier by the second. The fact that she's quiet now just means that we'll be in for a real horror later on. This is probably how Emperor Sutoku felt the first two or three days after being exiled to Sanuki.

I heard the sound of paper rustling and looked up. Asahina, who had been staring at her problem set across from me, held one finger to her lips and winked her right eye as she passed me one of the extra cards. Asahina then gave Haruhi a quick glance before taking her hand back. She looked back down like a little girl who had just succeeded in pulling off a prank.

I was fully intent on being an accomplice as I drew in the card Asahina had given me and took a look.

PLEASE WAIT IN THE CLUB ROOM AFTER WE'RE DONE. *MIKURU*

The message was written in small lettering.

Naturally, I'll do as she asks.

"That's it for today."

The second after Haruhi said that, she grabbed her bag and left the club room. It just felt so weird. A person that usually acted like a diesel truck that burned massive amounts of fuel was an admirable solar car today. Though it works out perfectly for me.

"Then I'll also excuse myself."

Koizumi put away the chess pieces and stood up. And after nodding to Asahina and me, he left the literary club room.

Nagato shut her book with a thud. Oh, you're going to follow them out? Thanks...and as I felt this sense of gratitude, Nagato walked over to me without making any sound, like a cat.

"Here."

She handed a piece of paper to me. It was another card. Handing me this thing doesn't mean I'm going to deliver it to the stars for you. And with that thought in mind, I looked down.

A number of unintelligible figures had been drawn on the card. What is this? The Sumerian alphabet or something? The Enigma machine wouldn't be able to decipher this thing.

My brow creased as I inspected these circles, triangles, and waves that really couldn't be considered pictographs or characters, and the next thing I knew, Nagato had spun around to pack up to go home and proceeded to trudge out of the club room.

Whatever. I slipped the card into my pocket and turned to Asahina, whom I had kept waiting.

"U-Um. There's somewhere I'd like you to come with me."

An invitation from none other than Asahina. I'd be struck by lightning if I turned her down. I'd jump into a blast furnace if she asked me to.

"Sure. Where are we going?"

"Um...That would be...Three years ago."

"Where" is what I asked yet "when" was the response I got. Still...

Three years ago. My initial reaction would be "Not again." But it managed to spark my interest. Which reminded me that Asahina is technically an unknown entity who claims to be a time traveler. She was so adorable that I'd completely forgotten. Still, three years ago? "That's where we're going? Which basically means time travel?"

"Yes—exactly."

"Well, I don't really mind, but why me? What are we going to do?"

"I'm sure that...you'll find out when you get there... probably."

What's that supposed to mean?

I must have shown traces of suspicion on my face. Asahina frantically waved her hands around with tears in her eyes as she begged me.

"I beg you! Please just say, 'Yes,' without asking anything for now. Or else I'll...well, be in big trouble."

"Uh. Okay then, I guess."

"Really? Thank you so much!"

Asahina happily jumped up and down as she clutched my hand. I mean, if Asahina is happy, so am I. Ha. Ha. Ha.

Thinking back, Asahina's confession that she had "come from the future" had, quite frankly, been based solely on her own word. The appearance of the other Asahina who looked all grown up had made me a believer, but I couldn't be positive that it wasn't some kind of trick. In that case, isn't this a perfect chance to see some proof to support the theory that Asahina is a time traveler?

"So, where's the time machine?"

I was expecting something along the lines of climbing into a desk drawer, but she told me that no such gimmick was involved. So how are we going to travel through time? Asahina fidgeted with her fingers in front of her apron.

"We'll go from here."

Huh? Here? I looked around the lifeless club room for no real reason. The two of us were alone.

"Yes, please sit down in the chair. Could you close your eyes? Yes, relax your shoulders."

I obediently followed her instructions. She wasn't going to whack me in the back of the head, right?

"Kyon..."

I could hear Asahina's hushed voice in my ear as she stood behind me. She breathed softly.

"I'm sorry."

I got a bad feeling and opened my eyes, which was when everything suddenly went dark. I experienced an overwhelming dizziness as I lost consciousness. As I completely blacked out, I thought for a second that maybe I should have refused.

When I regained consciousness, my vision was rotated ninety degrees. Things that should have been vertical were horizontal like the streetlight sticking from the left to the right, which made me realize that, yes, I was lying down. I soon discovered that the left side of my head felt especially warm.

"Ah, are you awake?"

The voice of an angel fully brought me out of my daze. What's that squirming under my left ear?

"Um...Could you lift your head soon or I'm going to be..."

Asahina said in a strained voice. I sat up and checked my surroundings.

I was sitting on a bench in the park at night.

I am at a loss for words. It would appear that I had been sleeping with my head in Asahina's lap. And since I had been asleep, I had no memory of the experience. What a waste.

"My legs are almost numb."

Asahina shyly smiled down at me. I have no idea where she'd gotten changed but she was wearing the North High sailor uniform instead of her maid outfit. I suppose that she'd had enough time to get changed since it appeared to be late in the evening. How long had I been asleep? And yeah, why was I asleep anyway?

"I didn't want to let you know how we time travel. Um, since it's classified... Are you mad?"

No way. Absolutely not. If Haruhi had been the one responsible, I would have punched her in the face, but since it was Asahina, I was totally fine with it.

In any case, one second I was sitting in a chair in the club room with my eyes closed, and the next thing I knew, I was in the park in the dead of night. And this park happened to hold a number of memories for me. This was the park where Nagato wanted me to come that one time. Was this like a mecca for weirdoes?

I scratched my head. There was something I needed to ask about first.

"What's the current date and time?"

Asahina, sitting next to me on the bench, replied, "July seventh, three years before the day we set off from. Around nine PM I think."

"For real?"

"For real."

She had a serious look on her face.

That was awfully simple. But I'm not naive enough to take

everything she says at face value. I need some kind of confirmation. Maybe I should check the time.

I was about to mention this when I suddenly noticed a weight on my left shoulder. I flinched. Asahina's head rested on my shoulder. A sound-asleep Asahina was leaning on me. What exactly does she mean by this?

"Asahina?"

No response.

"Excuse me..."

"Zzz..."

Zzz?

I turned my head about eighty-five degrees to the left to find Asahina with her lips half-parted and breathing softly as she slept. What the what?

Rustle, rustle—

Out of nowhere, the bushes behind me began to rustle and my heart began to pound. What the what?

"Is she sound asleep?"

The person who spoke as she emerged from the dark foliage was...another Asahina.

"Ah, Kyon. Good evening."

It was the gorgeous version of Asahina. The Asahina who had developed in all sorts of places and was a number of years older than the one sleeping next to me. A young, beautiful woman who retained her adorability despite filling out in a positive way. I'd met her once before. As she walked toward us, she wore the same white blouse and tight deep blue miniskirt she had back then.

"He-he. From this perspective..."

The adult version of Asahina poked the sleeping Asahina's cheek.

"I look like a child."

Asahina (Big) reached her hand out to familiarly touch Asahina (Small)'s sailor uniform.

"Was this how I looked back then?"

As I felt Asahina (Small) softly breathing on my arm, I could only look up at Asahina (Big) in a daze without moving a muscle.

"It was her role to guide you to this point. It is my role to guide you from here on."

I stupidly attempted to question the smiling and voluptuous Asahina.

"Uh...What's going on here...?"

"I can't give you any details. Because they're classified. So I can only ask nicely."

I turned to look at the snoozing Asahina leaning against me.

"I put her to sleep. I couldn't allow her to see me."

"Why?"

"Because I didn't run into myself when I was at this point in time."

Reasoning that sort of made sense, but not really. The alluring Asahina winked at me.

"If you follow those train tracks south, you'll come across a school. A public middle school. I want you to assist the person you find there. Could you go right away? As for the other me, sorry, but could you carry her there? She shouldn't weigh very much."

She sounds like a villager in some role-playing game. "What kind of item will I get in return?"

"What will you get in return...? Let's see, hmm—"

The adult version of Asahina tapped her finely shaped chin as she stood deep in thought before smiling knowingly.

"I can't personally offer you anything. However, you can kiss the me that's sleeping over there, but nothing more. And only while she's asleep, okay?"

Very attractive terms. Enough to make me want to pump my

fist. The sight of Asahina sleeping was lovely enough to make me lose control. But...

"That's a bit..."

It goes against my policy, both mentally and circumstantially. This is when I really start to hate my rational personality.

"It's time. I have to go."

That's all the advice I get this time?

"Oh, and please keep me a secret from her. Promise, okay? Want to pinky swear?"

Asahina (Big) stuck out her pinky and I unconsciously hooked mine with hers. We stood there like that for about a minute.

"Good-bye, Kyon. I'll see you again."

And with that bright farewell, Asahina (Big) walked off into the darkness, disappearing out of sight in no time. She had no trouble leaving this time.

Well, I thought to myself. I wonder how much time has passed for the adult version of Asahina since she last saw me. It didn't seem like she'd changed at all since our previous encounter when she'd given me that bizarre hint. Perhaps this Asahina was from an earlier time than the previous one. I have no idea. I had no way of knowing. The only thing I did know was that I'd be running into the Asahina from a different time period again.

I carried Asahina on my back and she wasn't exactly light, but at the same time, I wouldn't say she was heavy, so she was somewhere in between the two. Naturally, my steps began to slow. I'd be inclined to blame the innocent-looking face that was softly breathing into my ear. The back part of my neck she'd been breathing on was all itchy.

I did my best to avoid being seen by any people walking by as I followed the directions from the adult version of Asahina. I must have walked for approximately ten minutes through an increasingly uninhabited area. I turned a corner to arrive at my destination.

East Middle School. A place I knew as Taniguchi's and Haruhi's old school. Speaking of which, a familiar-looking person was clinging to the school gate. I couldn't possibly mistake the small shadow who was attempting to climb the metal gate.

"Hey."

I began having doubts upon opening my mouth. The fact that I could recognize this person was quite a mystery, if I do say so myself. I could only see this person's back and she was noticeably shorter. Her straight, black hair was at a length that couldn't be classified as long or short.

Maybe it was because I couldn't think of any other acquaintances who would be determined to climb over the school gate late at night.

"What is it?"

I was finally starting to feel like I had gone back three years in time. In fact, I actually had gone back in time.

The face that turned to look at me while she remained clinging to the gate was definitely younger than the face of the SOS Brigade chief I knew. But there was no doubt that those shining eyes belonged to Haruhi. The fact that she was haphazardly dressed in a T-shirt and shorts didn't make any difference. At this point, three years ago, Haruhi was a first-year in middle school. Was she the one Asahina wanted me to assist?

"Who are you? A pervert? Kidnapper? Awfully suspicious."

The hazy glow of the streetlight illuminated the surrounding area. I couldn't read the minute expressions on her face, but the middle school first-year Haruhi was obviously glaring at me as though I was a suspicious person. Between her sneaking into school in the dead of night and my wandering around carrying a sleeping girl on my back, which would be considered more suspicious behavior? There's a question I don't really want to think about.

"What are you doing here then?"

"Isn't that obvious? I'm trespassing."

You don't have to announce your criminal activities to the world. There are times when you shouldn't be aggressive.

"Perfect timing. I don't know who you are, but if you've got time, give me a hand. Or I'll call the cops."

I should be the one calling the cops on you. Still, I made a promise with the other Asahina. But yeah, I go back in time and I still have to deal with Haruhi Suzumiya.

Haruhi hopped down from the gate and opened the padlock on the bar. "Why do you have the key?"

"I stole it when I had the chance. Piece of cake."

That totally makes you a thief. Haruhi slowly slid the metal school gate open and beckoned me inside. I approached the girl, who stood about a head shorter than she would be in three years, and readjusted my hold on Asahina.

As soon as you passed through the main entrance to East Middle School, you would be on the school grounds and the school building was located beyond. Haruhi began walking across the dark grounds in a diagonal direction.

It's a good thing that it's dark. She won't get a clear look at my face or Asahina's this way. Certainly, Haruhi had never entertained the notion that she'd run into Asahina and me back during her first year of middle school, so we needed to keep it that way.

Haruhi headed straight toward the corner of the sports ground, leading me behind the athletic storeroom. A rusty cart, a rickety, wheeled field line marker, and a few bags of lime lay piled on the ground.

"I took this stuff out of the storeroom earlier this evening and

hid them here. Great idea, right?" Haruhi bragged as she piled bags of powder, which appeared to weigh as much as she did, onto the cart and lifted the handle. She looked like a child as she struggled to push the cart along. Guess a first-year in middle school might as well be a child.

I carefully set the slumbering Asahina against the storeroom wall. Please stay asleep for the time being.

"I'll take care of it. Hand it over. You take the line marker," I said.

Perhaps I shouldn't have acted in such a cooperative way. Haruhi abused me in such a frenzy that she'd have worked a rampaging robot to the bone if she'd been given the option. Her personality hadn't changed the least bit. I can see that her inner character didn't mature over the next three years.

"Draw the lines exactly the way I tell you to. Yes, I'm talking to you. I have to stand a ways away to supervise your line drawing to make sure you're doing it right. Ah, that spot's crooked! What are you doing?!"

Her ability to scream commands at a high schooler she'd never met before made it clear that Haruhi had always been Haruhi. If this had been my first encounter with this middle school girl, I would have thought that she was genuinely dangerous.

Before I met Nagato, Asahina, and Koizumi, at least.

There were no run-ins with teachers on night watch or police cars showing up after some nearby resident called the cops. For thirty minutes, I drew white lines in every direction on the school grounds per Haruhi's instructions.

I never would have thought that mysterious message that had suddenly appeared on the school grounds had been drawn by me.

As I stared in silence at the patterns I had painstakingly drawn,

Haruhi walked over next to me and took the field line marker from me. She proceeded to make a number of fine-tuning adjustments by adding a few lines here and there.

"Say, do you think aliens exist?"

That came out of nowhere.

"Why not?"

Nagato's face popped into my mind.

"What about time travelers, then?"

"Well, I wouldn't be surprised if they existed."

I'd be considered a time traveler myself right now.

"And espers?"

"Walking all over the place, I'd guess."

I recalled the countless number of red lights.

"Sliders?"

"I haven't met one of those yet."

"Hmm."

Haruhi tossed the field line marker aside and used her shoulder to wipe the dust off her face.

"Oh, well."

I was getting nervous. Don't tell me that I said something wrong. Haruhi looked at me with upturned eyes.

"That's a North High uniform, right?"

"Sure."

"What's your name?"

"John Smith."

"...Are you stupid?"

"Let's just say that it's my desired pseudonym."

"Who's that girl?"

"My older sister. She suffers from an erratic sleep disorder. It's a chronic disease. She falls asleep suddenly, so I have to carry her."

"Hmm."

Haruhi bit her lower lip and turned to the side with a look that said she didn't believe me. Let's change the subject.

"What is this supposed to be?"

"Can't you tell? It's a message."

"To whom? Don't tell me it's to Orihime and Hikoboshi."

Haruhi looked surprised.

"How'd you know?"

"Well, it is Tanabata. I just happen to remember someone doing something similar."

"Huh? I'd love to meet that person. There's someone like that at North High?"

"Sure."

You're the only person now and in the future who'll ever be like that.

"Hmm. North High, huh?" Haruhi murmured as she appeared to contemplate something. After staying as silent as a rock for a period of time, she abruptly turned around.

"I'm going home. I accomplished my objective. See ya."

And then she stomped off. She didn't even thank me for helping her. Extremely rude behavior, but that's what I'd expect from Haruhi. And she never told me her name either. Though that works out better for me, I'd say.

I couldn't stay in this place forever so I attempted to wake Asahina up. This was after I'd returned the cart and lime stolen by Haruhi to the spot behind the storeroom.

The sight of Asahina sleeping like a kitten was enough to make me lose control, but I resisted those urges and lightly shook her shoulder.

"Mmm...Hmm. Huh? Wha—"

Once Asahina had opened her eyes, she began looking all around.

"Wha-Wha—!"

She stood up.

"Wh-Wh-Wh-Whe-...Where am I? What how when are we right now?!"

How am I supposed to respond? As I racked my brain for an answer, Asahina emitted a short gasp before staggering. Even in the darkness, I could tell that her face had turned pale.

Asahina began searching herself with both hands.

"My TPDD...is gone. It's gone."

Asahina looked like she was about to cry. Soon enough, she really was crying. She looked like a little girl as she cried with her hands to her eyes, but it appeared that this wasn't the time to be in high spirits.

"What's a TPDD?"

"Sniff...That would be considered classified...It's kind of like a time machine. That's what I used to come to this time...but I can't find it anywhere. We can't return to our original time without it..."

"Uh, why is it gone?"

"I don't know...It should have been impossible to lose...Yet I lost it."

I recalled the other Asahina touching this one's body.

"Maybe somebody will come save us—"

"That's impossible..." she sobbed.

Asahina began explaining as she continued to sniffle. Established events on the time plane were supposed to be predetermined, so if a TPDD were to exist, it would be on her person. The fact that it was gone would be an established event, which would mean that its "absence" had been predetermined...and yeah. I don't get it.

"So in other words, what's going to happen to us?"

She sobbed, " In other words, we're stuck. We'll be stranded on

76

this time plane, three years in the past, unable to return to our original space-time."

We're in big trouble, was how I felt in my heart, but I didn't feel nervous at all. The adult Asahina hadn't given me any particular warning about this situation. She was probably the one who swiped the TPDD or whatever and created the current predicament. I presume that Asahina (Big) came to the past for that very purpose. An established event, right? From the perspective of the Asahina who came from farther in the future than this Asahina, it was predetermined.

I looked away from the sobbing Asahina to glance across the school grounds. The baffling jumble of white lines designed by Haruhi and drawn by me was sprawled across the field. The East Middle School staff and students who had no idea what had transpired would probably find this creepy when they showed up tomorrow. I'll just have to pray that there aren't any aliens out there who would consider this an insult...and that's when I had a sudden revelation.

After all, it'd been dark. The only lighting in the school was provided by a few flickering streetlights and the mess of white lines had been large in scale, so I couldn't tell what the whole thing looked like until I was a fair distance away.

Which is why it took me so long to notice.

I pulled the card Nagato had given me out of my pocket. The one with a number of unintelligible figures on it.

"There might be a way," I said as Asahina looked at me in tears. I continued to stare at the card.

The drawings on that card were exactly the same as the ones Haruhi and I had scribbled all over the school grounds.

After leaving East Middle in a hurry, we came to a stop in front of a fancy apartment in front of the station.

"Is this...Nagato's home?"

"Yes. I never heard any specific details about how long she'd been on Earth, but knowing her, she should have been on this world three years ago...probably."

I pressed the button for Room 708 on the intercom at the apartment's entrance. There was a buzzing sound to let us know somebody had picked up on the other side. I could feel the warmth of a trembling Asahina's hand through my sleeve as I spoke into the mic.

"Is this Yuki Nagato's residence?"

"..." was the response through the intercom.

"Ah—How should I put this..."

"..."

"Would it help if I were to say that I'm an acquaintance of Haruhi Suzumiya?"

I could feel a chilling presence on the other side of the intercom. There was a brief period of silence. Then...

"Come in."

There was a click as the door unlocked. I got into the elevator with the nervous Asahina in tow. We rode it to the seventh floor as our destination was Room 708, the one I'd previously visited while in the future. As soon as I rang the doorbell, the door opened, albeit slowly.

Yuki Nagato stood inside. This suddenly felt surreal. Had Asahina and I actually traveled to the past?

I had to wonder because Nagato looked exactly the same. The fact that she was wearing a North High uniform, the way she impassively stared at me, and even her inorganic appearance, which seemingly had no body warmth or presence, added to the impression that she was exactly the same as the Nagato I knew. However, there was something this Nagato had that the more recent one didn't. The glasses she had been wearing when I first met her.

The glasses Nagato had worn before she had stopped being a glasses girl at some point were sitting on this Nagato's face.

"Yo," I said as I raised one hand and gave a friendly smile. Nagato, as always, showed no expression on her face. Asahina was trembling as she hid behind me.

"Can we step inside?"

"..."

Nagato silently walked into the room. I took that as a yes and entered with Asahina. We took off our shoes and headed toward the living room. The room was as empty as it would be in three years. Nagato stood still, waiting for us to enter the room. I had no choice but to remain standing as I attempted to explain our situation. Where do I even begin? From the first day of school when I met Haruhi? That'll take a while.

I gave her a general rundown, abridging various spots. I must have spoken for five whole minutes as she impassively stared at me through her glasses. A summary of Haruhi's story that lacks any real point, if I do say so myself.

... "And so. The you from three years later gave this to me."

Nagato scrutinized the card I presented without batting an eye and traced her finger over the weird characters. Kind of looked like she was reading a bar code.

"Understood."

Nagato simply nodded. Seriously? Wait, hold on. There was something else that bothered me.

I put my hand on my forehead as I did some thinking.

"I've known Nagato for a while now, but three years ago ... Today for you ... So in other words, the present you. Today would have been the first time you met us, right?"

I have to admit that I had no idea what I was saying. Nevertheless, Nagato responded as the edges of her glasses flashed. In a calm and indifferent voice she answered.

"Yes."

"And so..."

"Requesting permission to access the memory corresponding to my time-divergent variant. I have downloaded reversible border regression data."

No idea what you're talking about.

"The 'me' in three years and the 'me' at this time are the same person."

"So? Of course you're the same person. That doesn't mean the Nagato from three years ago would share memories with the Nagato from three years later."

"We do now."

"How?"

"We have synchronized."

Yeah, I don't get it.

Nagato removed her glasses without any further response. She looked up at me with her emotionless eyes and blinked. That was definitely the familiar face of the book-loving girl. The Yuki Nagato I remembered.

"Why are you wearing a North High uniform? Did you already enroll?"

"I have not. I am currently in standby mode."

"Standby... You're going to stand by for three whole years?"

"Yes."

"That's just..."

That'll take a world of patience. Won't you be bored? But Nagato shook her head.

"That is my role."

She stared directly at me with clear eyes. "There is more than one method of time travel." Nagato spoke in a flat voice.

"The TPDD is merely a device for controlling time. Both unreliable and primitive. There are a number of theories concerning the process of movement through the time continuum."

Asahina squeezed my hand again.

"Um…What exactly do you mean…"

"When transportation of organic life forms is conducted with the TPDD, noise may occur. We believe it to be imperfect."

By we, she means the Data Overmind, right?

"You're capable of perfect time travel?"

"The process does not matter. The transfer of identical data suffices."

"Going from the present to the past or to the future, huh…"

If Asahina can do it, maybe Nagato can do it too. I assume that Nagato's the one with an excess abundance of power. In fact, after doing some comparing to Nagato and Koizumi, I'm starting to suspect that Asahina's the one who really has no idea what's going on.

"That's nice and all."

I interrupted Asahina and Nagato. "Now isn't the time to be discussing the finer points of time travel. We need to figure out how Asahina and I are going to get back to the future three years later."

However, Nagato simply nodded.

"It is possible."

She then stood and opened the sliding door that led to the room next to the living room.

"Here."

It was a Japanese-style room. With tatami flooring. The fact that the room was completely empty except for the tatami mats was what you would expect from Nagato, but why were we being shown into this guest room? Could there be a time machine hidden in here? As I wondered, Nagato removed a futon from the closet and spread it on the floor. And then a second one.

"I'm pretty sure I've got the wrong idea…but are you telling us to sleep here?"

Nagato, still carrying a futon, turned to look at me. I could see Asahina and myself reflected in her amethyst eyes.

"Yes."

I glanced next to me to find Asahina fidgeting with her face completely red. That's how I'd expect her to react.

But Nagato didn't seem to care.

"Sleep."

Don't be so direct.

"Just sleep and nothing else."

Well…That was the plan. In any case, Asahina and I looked at each other uncertainly. Asahina's face was bright red while I just shrugged. We had no choice but to rely on Nagato in this case. If she's telling us to sleep, then that's what we'll do. Just hope that it's as simple as waking up in the morning to find ourselves back in our world.

Nagato reached toward the switch on the fluorescent lamp next to the wall. Then she muttered something. I was wondering if she was saying good night when the light disappeared with a click.

It appeared that I had no choice but to sleep so I pulled the covers over myself.

And the next thing I knew, the light turned on. The fluorescent lamp made clicking sounds as it flickered and stabilized. Huh? Something feels wrong here. It was still dark outside.

As I sat up, Asahina also woke up, clutching the edge of her blanket.

The expression on her lovely, childlike face was one of bewilderment. She looked at me questioningly, but naturally, I had no answers.

Nagato was standing there. She had her hand on the light switch, just like before.

It didn't seem like Nagato's face. I could feel some emotion as I stared at the pale face. Like she had something she wanted to say but was unable to because of conflicting interests. It was the slightest expression of emotion that couldn't be perceived without being accustomed to her poker face for a long period of time. Though I couldn't be sure that I wasn't just imagining things.

I heard someone suddenly inhale next to me and turned to find Asahina fiddling with the digital watch on her right wrist.

"Huh? No way...! What? Really?"

I glanced at her wristwatch. "Don't tell me that thing's the TPDD."

"It isn't. This is just an atomic watch."

"One of those watches that synchronizes with the atomic clock through radio waves, huh?"

Asahina smiled cheerfully as she continued, "It's wonderful. We've returned. It's just past nine PM...on July seventh, the day we departed. I'm so relieved...Whew."

She sounded like the world had just been lifted off her shoulders.

The Nagato standing at the entrance was our Nagato. If you were going to differentiate between them by saying one was bespectacled and one wasn't, this one would be the latter. The Yuki Nagato who'd softened just a little bit. I could tell after seeing how she was three years ago. The Nagato before me right now had definitely changed from the Nagato I'd met in the literary club room when Haruhi dragged me there. I'm guessing it was so slight that she couldn't tell.

"But how?" Asahina asked in a daze.

Nagato responded in a flat voice, "I froze liquefied data within the selected space-time and unfroze the data once there were corresponding points from an already known space-time continuum."

Was that even comprehensible? After a brief pause, she added, "Which would be now."

Asahina attempted to stand before falling to her knees.

"You couldn't have...Impossible...How could you...Nagato, you..."

Nagato remained silent.

"What do you mean?" I asked.

"Nagato—stopped time. She probably stopped time for the whole room we were in, for three whole years. And then at this time today, she unfroze us...?"

"Yes," Nagato confirmed.

"That's unbelievable. She stopped time...Whoa..."

Asahina sighed as she remained bent over. That's when I thought of something.

It appeared that we had safely returned to our time three years later. After seeing Asahina's reaction, that was certain. She's incapable of hiding anything. Which is fine. The theory behind our return from three years ago involved stopping time—I can believe that. I have developed enough tolerance to accept just about anything at this point. That's fine too. Just fine and dandy—but.

This wasn't my first visit to Nagato's home. I'd been invited inside just a little over a month ago. But I stayed in the living room the whole time and never entered the guest room. I didn't even know about its existence. Which means, uh...What does it mean?

I looked at Nagato. Nagato looked back at me.

—So basically, when I visited this place to hear her crazy spiel, another me had been sleeping in the next room.

What the hell? Isn't that what this means?

"Yes," Nagato replied. I felt dizzy.

"...Hey. So in other words, you already knew everything back then? About me? About what happened today?"

"Yes."

From my perspective, my first meeting with Nagato had been on that day in the season of newly green leaves when Haruhi came up with the idea of establishing the SOS Brigade. However, Nagato had met me earlier, on Tanabata three years ago. As far as I was concerned, that meeting had occurred just a moment ago, but three years had passed since. I'm going to go insane.

Asahina and I stood in a daze together. I'd known that Nagato was capable of many things, but I never would have dreamed that she could stop time. Doesn't that make her invincible?

"Not exactly."

A motion of denial.

"This was a special case. An exception. Emergency mode. Rarely engaged. Unless drastic measures are required."

And we warranted those drastic measures.

"Thanks, Nagato."

I thanked her. That was all I could do.

"Not necessary."

Nagato nodded without a shred of amiability. Then she held out the card that had various geometric shapes on it. As I took the card, I noticed that the quality of the paper had deteriorated. As if it had been sitting there for three years.

"By the way, can you read what the writing on the card says?"

I didn't expect anyone to be able to read Haruhi's made-up message. So I was merely joking.

" 'I am here,' " Nagato answered.

I hadn't expected a reply.

"That's what it says."

I was getting confused.

"Don't tell me that...those pictographs or symbols or whatever actually ended up being the language of some alien race somewhere?"

Nagato didn't respond.

After Asahina and I left Nagato's room, we walked under the twinkling stars.

"Asahina, what was the point of me going back to the past?"

Asahina earnestly thought for a moment before looking up and speaking in a faint voice.

"I'm sorry. I, well...The truth is that, um...I don't really know...I'm at the bottom of the chain...No, a peon...No, something like an intern..."

"Yet you're close to Haruhi."

"That's because I never expected to be caught by Suzumiya."

She pouted as she spoke. Your face looks adorable like that, Asahina.

"I just follow orders from my superiors...or I mean, the people at the top. So I don't know the meaning behind my actions."

As I watched Asahina speaking bashfully, I wondered if those superiors included the adult version of Asahina. I had no basis for that assumption. It was simply because she and the normal Asahina were the only time travelers I knew.

"I see." I murmured, tilting my head.

I still don't get it. The adult version of Asahina had come to give me a hint, so she should have known what would happen to us. But she didn't tell anything to the present Asahina. What does that mean?

"Hmm."

After some groaning, I decided that there was no way for me to understand something Asahina didn't. Like Nagato said. There are many processes for time travel. Time travelers have their own rules and regulations to follow. Someone will explain it to me one day. When this is all over.

I parted ways with Asahina in front of the station. Her tiny figure bowed to me over and over as she reluctantly walked away. I also began heading home, which was when I realized that I'd left my bag in the club room.

The next day. Which would be July eighth. It felt like the next day to me, but physically, it'd been three years and a day since I'd gone to school. Empty-handed, I went straight to the club room, grabbed my bag, and headed to my classroom. I assumed Asahina had come before me since her bag wasn't there.

Haruhi was already in the classroom staring out the window with an impressed look on her face. Like she was ticking off the seconds before the arrival of aliens.

"What's wrong? You've been awfully melancholy since yesterday. Did you eat a poisonous mushroom or something?"

I sat down in my seat. Haruhi sighed in an exaggerated fashion.

"Not really. Just remembering something. The Tanabata season holds some memories for me."

I felt a chill down my spine. But I won't ask—what those memories might be.

"Really."

Haruhi turned back to stare at the clouds. I shrugged. I have no intention of playing with fire around a bomb fuse. That's how a person with common sense would act.

After school in the literary club room that had been turned into the SOS Brigade's hideout, Haruhi simply delivered the order, "Clean up the bamboo leaves. We don't need them anymore," and left. The "Brigade Chief" armband lying on the desk looks lonely. Oh, well. She'll be back to her usual crazy self tomorrow and telling us to do impossible things. That's the kind of person she is.

Asahina was nowhere to be seen. The only other people here were Yuki Nagato and Koizumi, who was playing chess with me. I'd given in to Koizumi's enthusiasm and allowed him to at least teach me how each piece was supposed to move.

It would seem that I'd been too quick to assume that he'd brought the chessboard because he was bad at Othello.

Koizumi was as bad at chess as he was at Othello.

As I took Koizumi's pawn with my knight, I glanced at the poker-faced Nagato, who was staring at the board with interest.

"Hey, Nagato. I can't really tell, but Asahina is actually from the future, right?"

Nagato slowly tilted her head.

"Yes."

"Still, the whole process of going to the past and coming back to the future didn't seem very consistent..."

Yeah. If time has no continuity—if we traveled three years into the past and then slept until the present time, the "present" we're in right now would be a different world from the "yesterday" we departed from. But in the end, I had given Haruhi unnecessary information and there was a possibility...that information had brought Haruhi to North High to search for nonhuman life...So it's possible that none of this would have happened if I hadn't gone three years into the past. Which means that there is continuity between the past and the future. That would contradict the explanation I'd heard from Asahina. I could at least figure that out by myself.

"Axiomatic set theory cannot prove the antinomies within itself without antinomies," Nagato said flatly.

I suppose you could say that she was showing emotion from a

relative standpoint. You may consider that an adequate explanation, but I have no idea what you just said.

Nagato exposed her pale throat as she looked up at me.

"You will understand eventually."

And with that, she returned to her usual position and began reading again. Koizumi started to speak in her place.

"It's like this. My king is currently in check by your rook. What a quandary. Where should it escape?"

As Koizumi spoke, he lifted his king and dropped it into his shirt pocket. Then he spread his arms like a magician.

"Well, was there anything inconsistent about my actions?"

I stroked a white rook as I considered his words. I had no intention of going along with his stupid Zen philosophy crap or abstract bull for the sake of compliments to satisfy my own vanity. So I didn't respond.

In any case— There's no doubt that Haruhi is made up of paradoxes. Same goes for this world.

"Of course, in our case, the king holds little value. What matters is the queen."

I placed the white rook on the square where the king had been. Queen's Knight 8.

"I have no idea what's going to be happening, but next time, I'd prefer to not have to use my head so much," Koizumi continued.

Nagato didn't respond and Koizumi merely smiled.

"I personally believe that some peace and quiet would be best, but would you prefer that something happen?"

I snorted as I marked a win under my name on the scorecard.

MYSTERIQUE SIGN

As expected, Haruhi had recovered from her state of melancholy and returned to doing whatever she wanted by the time term exams came around. As for me, I was totally depressed, as though Haruhi had passed the blue-colored baton of melancholy on to me. And I only felt worse every time a test was passed out. The only person who shared my melancholy was Taniguchi, probably. He'd been my buddy during midterms when we flew as close to the ground as possible while barely avoiding a lock from the radar called a failing grade. Humans are creatures who always want to be around people dumber than them. It makes you feel better, relatively. Of course, from an absolute standpoint, I didn't really have time to be feeling good about myself.

Haruhi, taking her test in the seat behind mine, somehow always finished with time to spare and could usually be found sleeping on her desk thirty minutes before time was up.

So annoying.

All clubs were on hiatus during term exams, so under normal circumstances, today would be the day clubs started meeting again, but for some reason, the SOS Brigade was in business year round and we'd met up yesterday and the day before that.

It appears that school policy doesn't apply to SOS Brigade activities. Obviously, since this whole thing has been wrong from the very beginning. This enigma of a brigade wasn't a club per se, so it didn't matter. That's Haruhi logic for you.

Like the other day. I'd finally gotten myself all psyched up to study, when at that very moment, Haruhi grabbed me by the sleeve and dragged me to the club room.

"Take a look at this."

Haruhi was pointing to the computer monitor she'd stolen from that other club a while back.

I had no choice but to look. A drawing program was open with some kind of scribble displayed. A circle around some letters that looked like drunken tapeworms. I couldn't tell if it was a picture or writing or both. This is what I would expect from a kid in preschool.

"What is this?"

I just spoke my mind.

Haruhi immediately puckered her lips like a duckbill.

"Can't you tell?"

"I have no idea. No idea at all. This thing makes yesterday's Modern Japanese test look easy."

"What are you talking about? The Modern Japanese test was really easy. Your little sister could have aced that thing."

That statement really pissed me off.

"This is the SOS Brigade emblem," she answered with a triumphant look on her face, as though she'd just accomplished something amazing.

"Emblem?" I asked.

"Yes. Emblem," Haruhi said.

"This is? It looks like something left by a drunken businessman, permanently stuck in a middle management position, who's on his way home from an all-nighter after working weekends for two straight months."

"Look closer. See? It says SOS Brigade in the center, right?"

When you put it that way, I can't say that I don't get the feeling that it does or doesn't, yet I wouldn't be confident enough not to refrain from voicing agreement. How many negatives did I just string together? I don't feel like counting, so if someone's free, tally them up for me.

"You're the one with the most free time. You probably won't even bother to study."

"I was fully intent on studying just a moment ago, but now that you mention it, it's true that I don't feel like bothering now."

"I'm thinking about putting this on the front page of the SOS Brigade's website."

Oh, yeah. We had a website. The worthless thing that only has a front page.

"We aren't getting any visitors. That's unacceptable. We haven't gotten any e-mails about mysterious happenings either. It's all because you got in my way. I was going to attract visitors with sexy pictures of Mikuru."

All pictures of Asahina as an earnest maid belong to me and I have no intention of letting anyone else see them. Some things in this world can't be bought with money.

"About the site you made, it's a lost cause. There totally isn't anything flashy on there. That's why I came up with this idea. To add a symbol of the SOS Brigade."

Delete that thing off the Internet already. I feel bad for anybody who accidentally visits such a stupid homepage. There are no contents so there's nothing to update. The whole site consists of the "Welcome to the SOS Brigade's website" image, a link to our e-mail address, and an access counter. And the access counter hasn't even reached three digits, and 90 percent of those hits came from Haruhi.

I watched as Haruhi opened a browser and loaded our amateur website.

"Why don't you write a journal or something? It's the job of the brigade chief to keep a log, right? The captain of a ship has to maintain a ship's log."

"No way. That sounds like a pain."

It'd be a pain for me too. If I were to attempt to describe a day in this place, I could only write about stuff like what book Nagato was reading or how I beat Koizumi at Five in a Row or how cute Asahina looked today or how Haruhi should sit down and keep her mouth shut. It wouldn't be fun to write and I doubt it'd be fun to read. Which is why I refuse to do something that wouldn't entertain a single person.

"Come on, Kyon. Put this symbol at the top of the page."

"Do it yourself."

"I don't know how."

"Look it up then. You're never going to learn anything if you turn to someone else every time you don't know something."

"I'm the brigade chief. The brigade chief's job is to give orders. Besides, if I do everything, you guys won't have any work to do. Try to use your head once in a while. You won't become a better person if you just do what you're told."

Are you telling me to do it or not to do it? Learn how to argue properly.

"Just do it already. I won't be fooled by your sophistry. Only bored Greeks during the BC era would appreciate that. Hurry it up!"

I really didn't want my ears to suffer any more of Haruhi's cawing like a crow at dawn, so I reluctantly opened the HTML editor and shrank master artist Haruhi's illustration, which looked something like a bored kid's scribbling, to an adequate size, pasted it onto the file, and uploaded the whole thing.

I refreshed the page to make sure it had worked. It appeared that the unwarranted SOS Brigade emblem had left its footprint on the Internet. A glance at the access counter told me that we were still in the double digits. I'm hoping that Haruhi's the only person checking this website. Since I don't want people to know that I was the one who made such a stupid site.

And with that side note, the first stage of my melancholy days comes to a close as a brief break begins tomorrow. This break is known as a post-exam vacation. A preparatory period for summer vacation during which teachers mark my test answers wrong.

Damn, this is annoying.

There was no point in feeling depressed about it, so I headed to the literary-club-room-turned-SOS-Brigade-hideout. At least I can ogle Asahina for some peace of mind.

Nagato would be reading in silence. Koizumi would be grinning as he solved shogi problems. Asahina would be waiting on everyone in her maid outfit. Haruhi would be talking and yelling and shouting about who knows what. My recent routine included having to listen to her bellowing.

I guess I shouldn't say recent when I suspect it's been like this since the beginning.

As I knocked on the door today, I started to get a sinking feeling. I was expecting a "Yes?" in Asahina's muffled voice, but I got something else instead.

"Come in!"

The greeting was delivered by Haruhi's casual voice, and I entered the room to find that she was the only one there. She had her elbows propped up on the brigade chief's desk as she fiddled with the computer she'd extorted from the computer society.

"Oh. It's just you."

"Yuki's also here."

Nagato was, in fact, sitting at the corner of the table with an open book, like a statue as always. She's like an accessory for this room so you don't have to include her. She never committed to joining the SOS Brigade either, and she's officially a member of the literary club. But I should still correct myself.

"Oh. It's just you and Nagato."

"Yeah, you have a complaint about it? I'm willing to hear you out. After all, I am the brigade chief."

"If I were to list out my complaints concerning you, I'd end up completely covering both sides of a sheet of legal-sized paper."

"I'm the one who feels disappointed. Knocking on the door made me think that a visitor had come to see us, you know. Don't confuse me like that."

I was taking extreme care so I didn't end up accidentally witnessing Asahina changing her clothes in the flesh. That lovable and careless person has been having a hard time remembering to lock the door.

And what do you mean by a visitor? Who's going to visit this place?

Haruhi turned to glare at me.

"Don't you remember?"

That made me jump. She couldn't be talking about what happened on Tanabata three years ago, right?

"You're the one who did it. Without obtaining my permission."

"What might you be talking about?"

"The poster you put up on the bulletin board in the clubhouse."

Oh, that. I breathed a sigh of relief.

She was talking about the fake club policy I'd made up to try to get the student council to accept the SOS Brigade. After concluding that a brigade which ran around looking for mysterious phenomena wouldn't have a chance, I indicated to the student council that the SOS Brigade should be allowed to continue as a sort of counseling group for all students. The executive committee called me an idiot and that was the end of that.

But I'd already made a poster. I don't really remember what I put on it, but it was probably something along the lines of "We'll listen to your problems." Since I'd already bothered making the thing, I stuck it up on a bulletin board that happened to catch my eye. After all, I assumed that it didn't really matter who saw this thing when there weren't any psychopaths who would seek counseling from the SOS Brigade. And it appeared I was right since we hadn't seen a single client yet, which was a very good thing.

Still, Haruhi had remembered this whole thing and been expecting clients to show up? I should probably go take that thing down on my way home. It'd get ugly if someone actually showed up with some kind of weird problem.

As I made this decision in the corner of my mind, Haruhi moved the mouse around.

"Anyway, look at this. Something's odd. Maybe the computer's acting up?"

I glanced past Haruhi's hair. The SOS Brigade's homepage was displayed spitefully on the monitor. But it was subtly different from the one I'd made. The crappy emblem Haruhi had drawn was distorted as though it'd been gathered like in sewing. And the counter and the title logo were just plain gone. I tried refreshing the page but nothing changed. It was like somebody had used a mosaic filter on the whole thing.

"It doesn't seem to be a problem with the computer. Looks like the file on the server is corrupt."

I wasn't that familiar with the Internet, but I at least knew that much. I happened to think of checking the version of the website stored locally, which loaded just fine in the browser.

"How long has it been like this?"

"Beats me. I've only been checking our e-mail the past few days so I haven't been on the website. It was like this when I looked today. Where do I direct my complaints?"

There's no need to complain to anyone. Just needs a simple fix. I took the mouse from Haruhi and overwrote the homepage file on the server with the one saved on this computer. Then I reloaded the page.

"Hmm?"

The site was still corrupted. I repeated the process a number of times but the result was the same. It appeared that we were dealing with a technical malfunction beyond my pay grade.

"Isn't this strange? Maybe it's one of those hackers or crackers I've heard about?"

"No way," I said. I really doubt someone would be bored enough to crack a site that nobody links to or visits. It must be some kind of error.

"Now I'm pissed. Is somebody committing cyberterrorism against the SOS Brigade? Who is it? If I find that person, I'll skip the trial and sentence him to thirty days of community service."

I turned away from the raging Haruhi to look at Nagato with her semblance of active camouflage. Maybe she can deal with this. I had this arbitrary image of Nagato being familiar with computers, but I'd never actually seen her using one. Actually, I should say that I've never seen her do anything besides read.

That was when someone knocked on the door.

"Come in!" Haruhi responded and the door opened to reveal Koizumi. He had the usual animated smile on his face.

"Oh. Now this is rare. Asahina has yet to show up?"

"Don't second-years have extra testing?"

The last day of finals for us first-years ended at third period. We could have gone home already, so why did we have to meet up in this place? Do I have no friends or something? And Haruhi, you're not going to give Koizumi the whole spiel about knocking on the door?

Koizumi set his bag on the side of the table as he pulled a Chinese checkers board from the cabinet and shot me an inviting glance. I shook my head, so Koizumi shrugged and began playing by himself.

I can't wait for Asahina's tea.

Knock knock.

Someone was knocking on the door again. I happened to be sitting at the brigade chief's desk as I struggled with an FTP program. Haruhi stood behind me and rattled off orders that were spontaneous and wrong, which meant I was forced to deal with her unreasonable demands.

Which was why the knocking on the door sounded like salvation to my ears.

"Come in!" Haruhi yelled again and the door opened. By process of elimination, it had to be Asahina.

"Ah, sorry about being late."

The person who apologized hesitantly upon appearance was none other than the wingless angel, Asahina.

"I had tests until fourth period..." she said by way of excuse when it wasn't necessary, as she hesitantly stood in the doorway. For some reason, she didn't enter the room and just stood there.

"Um, well..."

Everyone turned to look at Asahina. Once Asahina noticed that even Nagato was looking at her, she took a step back as though she were flinching before resolving to speak.

"W-Well...I brought a visitor."

The visitor's name was Emiri Kimidori. A second-year girl who appeared to be both soft-spoken and well groomed.

At the moment, the visitor was sitting with her head down in a chair, her eyes focused on the tea Asahina had poured. Asahina was sitting in a chair next to her. As you would expect, she hadn't changed into her maid outfit. A pity.

"So basically," Haruhi said, looking like an interviewer as she twirled a ballpoint pen. She sat across from the two second-years and spoke with a superior air.

"You want the SOS Brigade to look for your missing boyfriend, right?"

Haruhi balanced the pen on her upper lip as she crossed her arms. A gesture suggesting that she was deep in thought, but I knew better. She was just trying to hold herself back from bursting into laughter.

Man. I'd been all optimistic that we'd never get any visitors, yet here we were with our first counseling client. Haruhi probably wanted to jump with joy.

"Yes," Kimidori said to the teacup.

Nagato, Koizumi, and I were watching from the corner of the room. Haruhi looked at the two second-years.

"Hmm."

She hummed in an exaggerated fashion as she exchanged a look with me.

I was really starting to hate myself. I shouldn't have made that stupid poster. What'd I even put on it? Something about helping with the problems you couldn't tell anyone else...I think. Still, I didn't think any students would take it seriously. I mean, normally, you wouldn't, right?

Nevertheless, serious or not, Kimidori had seen the poster and had mistaken the SOS Brigade for a group that offered counseling for all students or performed odd jobs. I suppose that would be the literal interpretation of what I had written. Oh, now I remember. The club activities I'd made up had been "counseling

in regards to school life, consulting services, and participation in local volunteer activities." At the moment, the SOS Brigade had nothing to do with any of those activities. We hadn't done anything beyond messing up a baseball tournament.

Still, the stuff written on that poster had caught Kimidori's eye and alerted her to our existence, leading her to approach Asahina, who was in the same school year and brought her to this place. I suppose that's how it went.

As for her problem…

"He hasn't come to school for many days now."

Kimidori stared at the rim of the teacup as she spoke, refusing to meet anybody's eyes.

"He is rarely absent, yet he even missed a test day. Something must be wrong."

"Did you try calling him?" Haruhi asked. She was biting on the end of the ballpoint pen, maybe to prevent herself from cracking a smile.

"Yes. He doesn't answer his cell or his home phone. I went to his home, but the door was locked. Nobody answered the door."

"Uh-huh."

There's no denying that anybody who finds pleasure in the misfortune of others is a jerk, but Haruhi had such a strong aura of happiness about her that I was expecting her to burst into song any second. In other words, she's a jerk. Q.E.D.

"What about your boyfriend's family?"

"He lives by himself." Kimidori spoke to her cup. Apparently, it was her nature to talk to people without looking them in the eyes. "I heard that his parents live overseas. I don't have their contact information."

"Heh. Would they happen to be in Canada?" Haruhi said.

"No. I believe it was Honduras."

"Aha. Honduras, huh? I see."

What do you see? I doubt you even know where it is. Uh... Was it somewhere below Mexico?

"There wasn't any sign that he'd been in the room. It was completely dark when I visited at night. I'm so worried," Kimidori said in a forced voice as she covered her face with her hands. Haruhi pursed her lips.

"Hmm. I can understand how you feel."

Like hell you can. You couldn't possibly understand how it feels to be a girl in love.

"In any case, I'm surprised you came to see the SOS Brigade. Start by telling me your motive."

"Yes. He often mentioned you. That's how I knew about you."

"Huh? Who's your boyfriend?"

Kimidori murmured the name of a male student in response to Haruhi's question. I felt like I'd heard it before, but I didn't know anybody by that name. Haruhi's brow creased.

"Who is that?"

Kimidori spoke in a voice like a soft breeze.

"He mentioned being neighbors with the SOS Brigade."

"Neighbors?"

Haruhi looked up at the ceiling. Kimidori turned, looking at Asahina and me with our heads tilted before moving on to Koizumi and Nagato. But she never met our eyes and she then returned to staring at the teacup. Then she spoke.

"He serves as the president of the computer society."

And there you have it.

I had completely forgotten about that. That poor president, huh? The one who'd been photographed sexually harassing Asahina (against his will) and Haruhi had used that as leverage to acquire a top-of-the-line computer (by force). And to add insult to injury, the pitiful upperclassman who was the computer research society's president had even been forced to hook everything up while in tears. Wait, there's no need to feel sorry for him. If he has such a nice girlfriend, that makes up for pretty much anything. That's right. I wonder if the disposable camera we used was still sitting around somewhere.

"Yep, I got it!" Haruhi accepted readily. "We'll take care of it. You're in luck, Kimidori. As our first client, you get your problem solved free of charge as a bonus."

It won't be considered a school service if you charge money. Still, is there actually a problem for us to solve? Isn't it possible that the president merely turned into a *hikikomori*—a shut-in? I have no idea what his beef is when he's got a girlfriend like Kimidori, but I'm pretty sure he'll recover by himself eventually if you just leave him alone.

Of course, I didn't say any of that out loud. Kimidori left a slip of paper with her boyfriend's address before leaving the club room like a corporeal ghost.

Asahina had gone out into the hallway to see her off so I waited for her to return before opening my mouth.

"Hey, are you sure about accepting her request so readily? What if we can't solve her problem?"

Haruhi twirled the ballpoint pen around in good humor.

"We can do it. He's probably just cooped up with a two-month-late case of May sickness. We just have to march into his room, smack him around a few times, and drag him back here. Piece of cake."

It appeared that she actually believed what she was saying. Well, I felt the same way, more or less.

I asked Asahina, who was pouring us more tea.

"Are you friends with Kimidori?"

"No, I've never talked with her before. She's in the class next door so I've seen her during joint classes."

She could have gone to a teacher or the police instead of coming to us. Well, maybe she already talked to them. And they ignored her so she approached Asahina. That's probably how it went.

There was no sense of urgency as we sipped our tea. Haruhi appeared to be in unreasonably high spirits as she planned on accepting bigger requests and resolving them. Just stop.

Nagato closed her book with a thud and we proceeded with what Haruhi called an investigation.

The president lived in a studio apartment. Based on its location, I'd assume that most of the residents were college students. The three-story building wasn't great but it wasn't shabby either, and the paint looked good enough—it wasn't brand-new but it wasn't old either. An extremely ordinary place in appearance. Commonplace.

Holding the slip of paper with the address in her hand, Haruhi went up the stairs. The rest of us silently followed the summer uniform–clad figure.

"This is the place."

Haruhi checked the nameplate next to the metal door. The name Kimidori had given as her boyfriend's was inserted in the plastic casing.

"I wonder if there's a way to open it."

Haruhi rattled the doorknob a few times before pressing the button on the intercom. It should be the other way around.

"Why don't we circle around to the balcony in the back? We'll be able to get in if we smash the window, right?"

I'm praying that she's joking. This room is on the third floor and we aren't a bunch of juvenile delinquent thieves. I don't want a criminal record yet.

"Guess so. Let's go ask the landlord to lend us a key. If we tell him that we're worried about our friend, he should lend it to us."

Since you're good at pretending to be a friend. Still, the president lives by himself yet he never gave his girlfriend a spare key. That's like keeping the stem of an eggplant and throwing away the fruit.

Click.

Upon hearing a cold sound, I turned to find Nagato silently gripping the doorknob.

"..."

Nagato stared at me with eyes like liquid helium. She slowly pulled on the door and opened the entrance to the room. For some reason, the stagnant air inside created this chilling and lurking sort of feeling.

"Oh."

Haruhi's eyes were wide as saucers and her mouth was open in a half-circle.

"It was open? I didn't realize that. Well, whatever. Come on. Let's go inside. He's probably hiding under the bed or something. We'll drag him out and capture him. If he resists, you have my permission to kill him. We'll soak his head in beeswax and present it to the client."

Apparently, she didn't feel a single atom of guilt about stealing the computer. And we aren't dealing with Salome here. What's she going to do with a severed head?

She cheerfully pushed us all inside to find that the room was empty. Not even a single cockroach. Haruhi checked the bathroom and looked under the bed but there was nothing resembling a human being anywhere. The place was one fourth the size of the living room in Nagato's place but it had four times as much evidence of life. There was a bookshelf, a closet, something that looked like a small coffee table, and a computer rack all arranged neatly. We opened the window to check the balcony but there was only a washing machine hidden back there.

"That's odd."

Haruhi tilted her head as she bounced on the bed.

"I expected him to be curled up in a ball in some corner hugging his knees. Did he go to the convenience store? Kyon, do you know any other places a *hikikomori* might go?"

So it's settled that the computer society president is a *hikikomori*? Maybe he's on a vacation in Central or South America? Or is he actually trying to hide his whereabouts? We should have asked his homeroom teacher before coming here.

I had glanced at the computer-related books on the shelf when someone unexpectedly tugged on my shirt from behind.

"..."

Nagato expressionlessly looked up at me and shook her chin to the side. What's that supposed to mean?

"It would be best if we left," Nagato softly whispered. It was the first time I had heard her speak today. Haruhi and Asahina didn't notice, but Koizumi moved his face next to my ear.

"I concur."

Don't use a serious tone, Koizumi. You're freaking me out. But Koizumi merely flashed a forced smile while his eyes were somber.

"This room feels oddly discomforting. Similar to a sensation I am familiar with. Though it may only feel similar and be different fundamentally..."

Haruhi opened the fridge without permission, and said, "Found a yummy ice cream treat, *warabimochi*! It expired yesterday. Let's eat it so it doesn't go to waste," as she tore the bag open. Asahina was all flustered as Haruhi held out the convenience store pastry for her to taste test.

I also found myself speaking in a hushed voice.

"Similar to what?"

"Closed space. This room has the same scent as that place. No, I'm merely using the word 'scent' in a figurative sense. You could say it's a feeling, a sensation transcending the five senses."

I stopped myself as I was about to reflexively deliver a biting remark about being an esper or something. This guy actually is an esper. Now that I think about it.

Nagato murmured in a soft voice that barely shook the air, "A dimensional rift exists. Phase shift is transpiring."

Like that tells me anything.

Least, that's what I want to say. But my legs would probably turn to jelly if Nagato suddenly looked at me with a sad face, so I'm better off keeping my mouth shut. Good grief.

In any case, it appears that we should get out of here pronto. I motioned to Koizumi and Nagato before turning to Haruhi, who was devouring her treat.

Once everybody had left the apartment building, Haruhi said that she was hungry, so we were dismissed for the day and she left by herself. The case Kimidori had brought to us was temporarily shelved as Haruhi said irresponsibly, "It'll work itself out eventually," so all thinking ground to a halt and everything was on hold for the day.

I guess she's already lost interest.

Haruhi wasn't the only one who hadn't had lunch yet, but I only pretended to go home as everyone went their separate ways. After spending ten minutes waiting in an irritated mood, I returned to the entrance of the president's apartment building.

The other three brigade members had already assembled and were waiting for me. The logic-loving alien and the damn knowledgeable esper looked like they knew what was going on, unlike Asahina.

"Um…What's the matter? Why did you tell us to reassemble without Suzumiya noticing…"

She glanced up at me. She seemed uneasy when she looked at Nagato and Koizumi. I'll just assume that I was the one she'd been waiting for.

"Those two are concerned about the room we were just in," I answered. "Right?"

Smiley and Poker Face nodded at the same time.

"We should know for sure once we go back there. Right, Nagato?"

Nagato walked off without a word. The rest of us followed. Nagato walked up the stairs without making a sound, opened the door to the president's residence without making a sound, and removed her shoes without making a sound before proceeding to the center of the room.

The studio apartment wasn't particularly big since the four of us standing in a line took up the whole room.

"Within this room…"

Nagato began to speak.

"…an amalgamated alternate space-time with noncorrosive tendencies is occurring independently in a restrictive mode."

…

I waited for a bit, but that was the end of her explanation. What am I supposed to do when you sound like you just randomly picked out words from a dictionary?

"The sensation I'm experiencing is similar to that of closed space. The latter originates from Suzumiya, but the former gives off a different scent," Koizumi said as a follow-up to Nagato's explanation.

The two of you make a good combination. You should get together. Teach Nagato some hobbies besides reading.

"We can deliberate on this matter later. We have something more important to take care of at the moment. Nagato, the president's disappearance is a result of this abnormal space, correct?"

"Yes."

Nagato raised one hand in a gesture that looked like she was stroking the air before her.

A bad feeling raced up my spine and tickled my brain. I probably should have told her to wait. But before I had a chance to utter that syllable, Nagato was already murmuring something around that sounded like a tape playing at 20 × speed. And in a flash, the scene before me changed.

"Huh?!"

Asahina jumped over and wrapped herself around my left arm. But I had no time to enjoy the sensation against my arm. I was too busy trying to verify my current location.

Uh, I was in the president's cramped studio apartment. Not an eerie place like this. Not a place so wide and flat that you can't even see the horizon with an ocher brown mist hovering in the air. Who brought me to this place?

"Entry code analyzed. This place overlaps normal space. A phase has merely slipped off," Nagato explained.

Well, she's the only one capable of this stuff. And Koizumi's the only one who can hold any semblance of a conversation with Nagato.

"It doesn't appear to be Suzumiya's closed space."

"It is deceptively similar. However, a sector of the data in this space contains traces of junk data originating from Haruhi Suzumiya."

"How significant are these traces?"

"Of an inconsequent level. She was merely the trigger."

"I see. So that's how it is."

Asahina and I aren't part of this conversation. Not that it bothers me. In fact, I'm pretty grateful. Though I'd be more grateful if they could take us back to our world.

Asahina clung to me as she fearfully looked around at our surroundings. It appeared that she hadn't anticipated this space. I hadn't either, as I was also glancing in every direction. I could breathe fine, though I had to wonder if it was okay to breathe in this ocher mistlike stuff. I could feel the warmth of the floor through my socks. Not sure if this would be considered floor or ground, but the ocher surface continued infinitely. Didn't expect a standard-sized room to have this much storage space. An alternate dimension, huh? Well, I was expecting something like that to show up soon. I'm awfully composed, if I do say so myself.

"Is the computer society president here?"

"It would seem so. I would presume that this alternate space appeared in his room and trapped him within."

"Where is he? I don't see any sign of him."

Koizumi merely smiled as he turned to Nagato. I guess that was some kind of sign since Nagato raised her hand again.

"Wait!"

I wasn't too late this time. I directed my attention to Nagato, who had obediently frozen in place.

"Could you tell me what you're going to do first? I'd like a moment to prepare myself."

"Nothing."

Nagato responded as if she were a talking piece of glasswork as she tilted her hand up around seventy-five degrees and extended her index finger. And then she opened her mouth again.

"It has come."

I looked in the direction Nagato was pointing.

"Hmm."

I had to groan in spite of myself.

The ocher mist was slowly swirling into what looked like a whirlpool gathering each and every particle composing the mist into one spot. I was starting to feel like a pathogen that had invaded someone's body, since I was getting this image of the ocher whirlpool carrying out its duty like a white blood cell. My only comfort was the warmth of Asahina's hands.

"I can sense a clear intent of animosity," Koizumi said calmly, without any hint of urgency.

Nagato was standing still with her arm extended like a broken-down android. That didn't mean it was okay for me to relax. They might have the means to defend themselves, but I don't. Asahina doesn't either, which is why she's hiding behind me.

"This is when you're supposed to bring out some futuristic gadget. Don't you have like a ray gun or something?"

"Carrying weapons is prohibited. It's dangerous," Asahina answered in a trembling voice.

I can understand that. Even if you put a weapon in the hands of "this" Asahina, she would still be useless and prone to accidentally leaving it on the train. I began wondering if she might improve as she got older, but on second thought, "that" Asahina was also fairly careless. Maybe she's just a scatterbrain by nature.

While I was thinking, the mist was gradually taking the form of a solid object. There must have been some sort of reason for this. Not that I was particularly interested in knowing it, but for some reason, I could recognize the shape the mass of ocher was forming.

"Eek."

Asahina was the only one scared. I'll admit that it had a creepy appearance and you normally wouldn't come across one in town. The last time I'd seen one had been many years ago under the floor at my grandmother's house in the country.

Are you aware of an insect known as the cave cricket?

If you aren't, I'd like to show you what I'm seeing right now. You'll learn every small detail about it.

After all, this cave cricket looks like it's three meters long.

"What is this?" I asked.

"A cave cricket, I presume," replied Koizumi.

"That much I know. I used to be known as a bug expert when I was in preschool. I've never seen a real one before, but I know how to differentiate between a *Hexacentrus japonicus* and a *Mecopoda nipponensis*. But forget that. What is this?"

Nagato spoke softly. "The creator of this space."

"This thing?"

"Yes."

"Don't tell me this is Haruhi's doing again?"

"The cause lies elsewhere. But it began with her."

I was about to ask her what she meant when I noticed that she was still obediently frozen in the same position.

... "You can move now."

"Yes."

Nagato then lowered her arm and stared at the giant cave cricket that had materialized. The burnt brown sand treader was standing in a spot a few meters away from us.

"Oh? While imperfect, my power appears to be effective here."

Koizumi held a ball of red light the size of a handball in one hand. That red ball I'd never wanted to see again after the first time. It appeared to have come from his palm.

"My strength is one tenth of what it is in closed space. And I am unable to transform myself."

For some unknown reason, Koizumi turned to Nagato with that cheerful smile I was sick of seeing.

"Perhaps it was judged that this would be sufficient?"

"..."

Nagato didn't react. I repeated my question.

"Anyway, Nagato. What's the true identity of that bug? Where's the president?"

"It is a subspecies of data life forms. It is using the brain tissue of a male student to heighten the probability of its existence."

Koizumi tapped his finger against his brow. It seemed like he was thinking, but it also seemed like he was focusing his thoughts. Koizumi eventually looked up.

"Perhaps the president is inside that giant cave cricket?"

"Precisely."

"The cave cricket is…I see. The president's visualization of a source of fear, correct? Defeating it should cause this alternate space to collapse. Am I wrong?"

"You are not."

"I appreciate the metaphor that's easily understood. That should make this quite simple."

"No, it's not easily understood. No, this isn't simple. Explain everything so that Asahina and I know what's going on."

"We don't have time for that right now, though."

"Don't emphasize the last syllable like that. Stop smiling all gentle-like. Throw that red ball somewhere else. And do something about Asahina wrapping herself around my waist. I'm about to lose it."

"Eek…"

The trembling Asahina had taken away my ability to move. At this rate, I won't be able to escape

"That won't be necessary. It won't take long. I just know it some-how. This appears to be much easier than hunting Celestials."

The cave cricket had finished materializing and I was worrying about whether it would suddenly jump toward us. I wonder how many meters it can jump. I kind of want to measure…No, not really.

I was blunt.

"Get it over with."

"Roger that."

Koizumi launched the red ball and whacked it like he was serving a volleyball. The red handball flew off with impeccable accuracy as it crashed into the front of the cave cricket and made a sound like a paper balloon popping. A pretty stupid method of attacking, but our opponent appeared to be pretty stupid too. I was expecting some form of counterattack, but the cave cricket didn't run, jump, or make any weird roaring sounds. It just sat there in silence.

"Is it over?"

Nagato nodded in response to Koizumi's question. That didn't take long.

The giant cave cricket began diffusing into its original state of mist and started to fade. The ocher mist trembling around us also began to disappear. Along with the chilling sensation under my feet.

A male in a familiar uniform appeared as a form of compensation, I suppose. The president of the computer society collapsed faceup. He looked like he had fallen out of the chair in front of the computer rack as he lay there with his eyes closed. It appeared that he was alive. Koizumi leaned down next to him and placed one hand against the president's neck before nodding to me.

We were back in the room in the studio apartment. Makes you wonder where that huge space came from.

In any case, I'm feeling quite relieved. I've had enough of being trapped in wide-open spaces, whether they're gray or ocher.

"Approximately two hundred eighty million years ago."

Nagato began her explanation of random cosmic nonsense, which if I were to break it down and condense it, would turn into something like the following:

It was either during the Permian or Triassic period when "it" landed on earth, and at the time, there was nothing on Earth capable of housing "it." Lacking the means to exist on Earth, it went into hibernation to allow for self-preservation. Until an appropriate data network had been born on the planet for it to use.

It lacked the means to exist on Earth. Thus, it froze all activities and settled into a state of sleep.

Eventually, humans were born on Earth and those humans created computer networks. Such immature (according to Nagato) digital information networks, though imperfect, could be utilized as nurseries. However, those were insufficient, so that thing remained in a half-awakened state. But there was an incident which incited its awakening. What served as an alarm clock for that thing was a detonator floating across the Internet. It held more data than could be measured by ordinary numbers. Data that does not exist in this world. Data from another world. This was the shelter that thing had been waiting for...

Nagato abruptly stopped talking.

Nagato had been using the president's computer as she talked and brought up the SOS Brigade website and displayed the corrupted SOS Brigade emblem.

"The trigger was the invocation sign drawn by Suzumiya. It became a gate."

"So this SOS Brigade emblem turned into a summoning circle or whatever just now?"

"Yes." Nagato nodded. "By terrestrial standards, this SOS Brigade emblem holds the equivalent of approximately 436 terabytes of data."

That's impossible. That image isn't even 10 kilobytes big.

But Nagato continued, "It does not correspond to denominations used on Earth."

"What are the odds? A symbol she drew by chance happened to correspond perfectly. She truly is Suzumiya. She can even beat astronomical odds."

Koizumi was seriously impressed. And I was seriously scared. Scared of what?

Haruhi does most things on a whim. That's how the SOS Brigade was formed and that's how members were assembled. Asahina was picked up as a mascot character. Koizumi was chosen because he was a transfer student. Nagato had been there to begin with. And then, Asahina was a time traveler, Koizumi was an esper, and Nagato was a pseudo-alien. Too convenient. In fact, Koizumi had said that it wasn't coincidence when he gave me that nonsense about stuff happening because Haruhi so desired. I'd almost started to believe him, but I couldn't let that happen. After all, I am an utterly ordinary person. That should be enough to prove otherwise. Koizumi's theory would require me to have some kind of secret identity that involved hocus-pocus. So it would seem...

What if there had actually been a purpose behind Haruhi's pointless actions? A purpose she was unaware of. Like how she could randomly write down characters and create a message to some aliens out there. Like a cat tapping away at a keyboard and producing a legible sentence. What are the chances of that happening?

A girl who can easily break through the barrier called probability and unconsciously reach the correct answer. That would be the troublemaker known as Haruhi Suzumiya. I could accept her making me join the SOS Brigade to run errands for her. Yeah, that's right. It beats the hell out of me having some kind of mysterious background. So, do I have some kind of crazy unknown power or origin?

Is that why she chose me? Don't tell me that I actually have a secret I don't know about.

The next issue is what I'm truly frightened about.

Who am I?

I shrugged in an imitation of Koizumi. He's the one who says, "Good grief." I'm the one who's most aware of what my own role is. In short, I serve as the SOS Brigade's conscience. That has to be it. Deep down, I'm different from the other three brigade members. I'm in the SOS Brigade to persuade Haruhi to spend her time in high school in a normal fashion. It's my duty to make her give up and disband this illegal club. Now that I think about it, this would be the fastest path to a peaceful world. No, it's the only path.

It's a lot easier to change Haruhi's concept of the world than to turn the world into the kind of place Haruhi wants. Plus, it doesn't impose on anybody else.

Of course, the SOS Brigade may never have existed if I hadn't given Haruhi some bizarre inspiration. Well, you know, we should judge these things on a case-by-case basis. I'll work this out somehow. Though I don't know how long it'll take or why I'm the one that has to do this.

Let's just move on.

"So what was that cave cricket anyway?"

I figured that I needed to get that question answered before this ordeal would end. Nagato answered in a tone that was like exhaling carbon dioxide.

"A data life form."

"A relative of your patron?"

"Their origin was similar. However, they branched down a different evolutionary path and became extinct."

Except there ended up being a survivor. It didn't have to hibernate on Earth of all places. It could have gone to sleep somewhere around Neptune.

To think that the development of the Internet would become a breeding ground for pseudo-evil gods. That's when I thought of something. I turned to the petite upperclassman who was collapsed on the floor.

"Asahina, how advanced are the computers in the future?"

"Huh…"

Asahina opened her mouth before shutting it again. I hadn't really been expecting an answer since it was probably classified, but someone else responded.

"Such a primitive form of data network should no longer be in use," Nagato said as she ruined the mood and pointed to the computer.

"It is simple to create a system that does not rely on storage media, even for organisms such as terrestrial humans."

Nagato turned to the side to look at Asahina, who visibly paled.

"Really?"

"That's...um..."

Asahina mumbled as she hung her head.

"I can't say..." she said in a quivering voice. "I don't have the authority to confirm or deny that. I'm sorry."

It's totally fine. There's no need to apologize, seriously. I wasn't that interested in finding out—hey, Koizumi. How dare you have such a disappointed look on your face?

I attempted to change the subject to save Asahina. Uh, what was there to talk about again? That's right.

"There's still something odd."

I waited for everybody to turn their attention to me.

"I was with Haruhi when she was viewing the stupid picture, and nothing happened. Besides, shouldn't that thing have shown up the second Haruhi finished her drawing?"

Koizumi gave the response.

"That club room had been transformed into alternate space long ago. A variety of elements and force fields battled and negated one another, leaving the room relatively normal. You could say that it's in a saturated state. The room is already filled to capacity with various things so there is no room for further assimilation."

What kind of logic is that? And when had the club room been turned into a den of evil? I never noticed.

"Ordinary people aren't equipped with unnecessary sensory capabilities. Yes, it's safe to assume it to be harmless. Most likely."

Good grief. I wouldn't mind the temperature of the room being lowered a bit during summer, but if it gets to the point where I start searching for a hanging rope, I'm out.

"You shouldn't have to worry about that. Nagato, Asahina, and I are working hard to prevent that."

"Are you sure this isn't the result of your hard work?"

Koizumi smiled and said, "Who knows?" as he tilted his head and spread his arms with his palms facing upward.

I turned back to the computer screen. As I stared at the corrupted SOS Brigade symbol, I noticed something. I scrolled down to the bottom of the page.

"Bah."

The access counter was showing. For some reason, it was the only normal part of the website as it displayed the number of visitors. The access counter hadn't even been three figures the last time I checked. At the moment, the counter for the SOS Brigade website was at ten, a hundred, a thousand... Whoa, it was almost up to three thousand. Who's looking at this thing?

"Hyperlinks have been placed in various places," Nagato said in a quiet voice.

"That is how this data life form multiplies. Very immature. Its data is copied into the brains of the humans who see the signs, leading to the creation of restricted space. A large number of people are required."

"Which means everybody who saw this... Almost three thousand other people are in the same predicament as the president was?"

"Not exactly. The data for the summoning emblem is damaged. Only a few people browsed the correct data source."

Probably a server error. Either way, that's a big help.

"So how many idiots out there clicked the suspicious link and saw the real thing?"

"Eight. Five are students at North High."

Then those eight people are also trapped in that ocher space-time.

That space controlled by a metaphor that might not necessarily be a cave cricket. We should help—or yeah, we have to go save them. Koizumi was asking Nagato for their addresses (It doesn't surprise me that Nagato knows this information) and Asahina appeared to intend to go along with them. That means I have to go too. Most of the blame goes to Haruhi, but I was the one who put this magic circle-like thing on the Internet, so I should help clean up the mess.

So I can sleep soundly at night.

The victims at North High wouldn't be a problem, but it appeared that we'd have to ride the train to save the other three people.

Anyway.

The post-exam break was over with. All that remained was to sit in the club room and wait for summer vacation.

I told Haruhi that the president had come back to school.

"Hmph. I see."

And with that, she zipped out of the classroom. She was probably stuffing herself in the cafeteria by now. Koizumi and Asahina hadn't shown up yet.

By the way, Nagato had redone Haruhi's SOS Brigade symbol and I stuck it on the page. I managed to safely upload it this time. I wonder why? I hope that people concentrate when they look at this thing. The difference was ever so slight, but if you paid attention, you'd find that the drawing said ZOZ Brigade now. That tiny change was apparently the difference between weird stuff showing up or not.

I'd be inclined to say that the moral of this whole spiel would be, "Don't click on links you don't recognize." What do you think?

As I considered the matter, I looked at Nagato, who was sitting at the end of the table reading a numbered set of technical books.

As I watched Nagato's face, I suddenly thought of something. I don't know when she noticed Haruhi's summoning picture, but maybe she had been the one who destroyed the data?

And there was the person who brought this matter to our attention, Kimidori. I had just visited the computer society's club room and been told that the president didn't have a girlfriend. By the president himself, who appeared perfectly fine besides the fact that he didn't have any memory of the past few days. It didn't seem like he was lying as he gave me a clueless look when I mentioned Kimidori's name. The president isn't that good of an actor.

I became suspicious.

Had Kimidori really come here to request our help? The timing had been too perfect. Haruhi scribbled her drawing and I put it on the website. A number of people saw it and were taken by that data life form thing to an alternate dimension. That was when Kimidori came to us and told us her story and we went to the president's home. And then we exterminated it.

A perfectly scripted scenario and Nagato was always at the center of it. I wouldn't be surprised if the omnipotent alien terminal had gone so far as to manipulate Kimidori into bringing us this case.

She may have come up with the idea of a fake client to ease away some of Haruhi's boredom. If that were the case, Nagato could have dealt with it by herself without getting us involved. Is that what usually happens? She secretly prevents weird stuff from happening without saying a word, in silence, from the shadows.

A breeze came in through the window and ruffled Nagato's hair and the pages of her book. Her pale fingers gripped the edges of the book and her pale face was perfectly still as her eyes followed the text.

Or perhaps, Nagato brought us in because she wanted to? An alien-made organic android living for years in a totally empty room. Though she appeared to feel no emotion on the outside, perhaps she could.

Perhaps she still felt lonely when she was all by herself.

REMOTE ISLAND SYNDROME

I was so dumbfounded I forgot about the pain in my shoulder.

At the moment, I was lying on my belly, unable to stand as I couldn't help being astonished by the sight before my eyes. I was unable to move because of an excess amount of weight on my back that refused to budge. But that wasn't my concern at the moment. Koizumi, draped over me in the aftermath of breaking down the door, was also stunned by the scene in the room before us. Get off me already—but my mind wasn't clear enough to channel that thought. That's how shocked I was.

That which could never possibly happen had happened. It had actually happened. This could no longer be laughed off as a joke. What are we supposed to do?

There was a flash outside the window. A few seconds later, the rumbling of thunder reached my stomach. Just like yesterday, a full-blown storm was covering the entire island.

"It can't be," someone murmured.

It was Arakawa, who had been slamming against the door with Koizumi and me and fallen to the floor when it opened.

Koizumi finally got off me so I rolled over and sat up.

And then I took another look at the unbelievable sight before my eyes.

On the carpet near the door lay a man sprawled on the floor the way I was a moment ago. A resident of this manor who hadn't come down to the dining room this morning and also happened to be our host, a man in his prime. I could immediately identify him because he'd been wearing the same clothes when he'd left us in the living room last night and headed upstairs. He was the only one wearing a formal suit in this hot weather on an island when there was no need for it. He was also the employer of Arakawa, who had been murmuring a moment ago, and the owner of this island and manor...

Mr. Keiichi Tamaru.

Keiichi was lying on the floor with a look of astonishment on his face. He wasn't moving a single muscle. Of course he wasn't. Since it appeared that he was already dead.

How did I know? It was obvious. The item protruding from his chest looked familiar. It was the handle of the fruit knife that had been included with the bountiful fruit basket we had been served during dinner.

I'm willing to bet that you'd find a metal blade on the other side of that handle. Or else, it wouldn't be sticking out of the chest of an unmoving human who had his eyes and mouth wide open. Which meant that the knife was stuck in Keiichi's chest.

I'm pretty sure that most people would die if they had a knife through their heart.

And that would describe Keiichi's current state.

"Eek..."

I heard a soft shriek of terror from the other side of the busted door. I turned around. Asahina stood with her hands over her mouth. She staggered backward but Nagato was there to support her from behind. Nagato turned to me with her permanently blank face and lifted her head as if deep in thought.

Naturally, she could always be found where we were.

"Kyon, could it be that...this person is..."

Haruhi also looked surprised. Her head was sticking into the room next to Asahina as she stared at Keiichi in eternal repose with catlike eyes in the darkness.

"Dead?"

Her voice was unusually soft and even slightly nervous, which was very peculiar. I turned around to try to say something. Koizumi's usual smile was nowhere to be found as he had a somber expression on his face. The maid, Mori, was also standing out in the hallway.

Only one person who'd been in the manor yesterday was missing from this scene.

Keiichi's younger brother, Yutaka Tamaru, wasn't here.

We broke into the room to find one silenced owner of the manor and one person who happened to be suspiciously absent. What might that mean?

"Hey, Kyon..."

Haruhi spoke again. It almost looked as though she were going to cling to me any second. She had an unfamiliar look of anxiety on her face.

Another flash of lightning lit up the room. The storm had peaked yesterday. The sound of thunder accompanied the crashing of waves in an array of goose bump–inducing sounds.

This was a remote island. And there was a storm. And the master of the manor was lying before us in what had been a sealed room, with a knife in his chest.

I couldn't help wondering.

Hey, Haruhi.

Were you the one who made this happen?

I flashbacked to the reason the SOS Brigade members ended up in this place.

Back one day before summer vacation had started...

....

......

...

It was mid-July in the dead of summer. The weather was so intensely hot that I wanted to give the sun a paid vacation.

As always, I was in the literary club room, which served as our hideout, drinking Asahina's trademark hot tea. I was attempting to recover from the term exam results we had just received, but when I thought about how I'd have to take supplementary classes, I couldn't really relax. This is when people start wanting to escape reality.

I spontaneously came up with a number of potential reasons for why reality was just a big lie and began mulling over which one to use.

"Um, is something the matter?"

I snapped myself out of the fake story where a bunch of evil aliens from the dark side of the moon would land and destroy the Diet building on the day before makeup exams.

"You have a strained look on your face...Does the tea taste bad?"

"Of course not."

It was as sweet as always. Though it was made using cheap tea leaves.

"That's a relief."

Asahina breathed a soft sigh as she stood in her summer maid outfit. I responded to her relieved smile with a smile of my own.

Your happiness is my happiness. You could send Xu Fu from China to the mountain gods of Mount Penglai in a quest for a miracle cure and not find a panacea stronger than Asahina's smile. My heart currently felt clearer than the surface of Lake Mashu, and I swear that I could almost envision messengers from heaven blowing on their horns...

And I was in the middle of delivering an impassioned speech like Saint Francis of Assisi preaching to the birds but I stopped. Not because I got sick of chaining modifiers, but because someone showed up to interfere with his needlessly melodic voice.

"Hello, everyone. How did you do on your finals?"

Koizumi rolled the dice on the Monopoly board on the table as he asked the question he really didn't need to ask. Thanks to him, my mind was warping to the dark side of the moon again and was in satellite orbit before I could calm myself down. Why don't you just play Monopoly by yourself over there? Learn a thing or two from Nagato, who's sitting in the corner of the room and quietly reading a book.

Nagato had what looked to be a hardcover encyclopedia open as she sat in a metal folding chair in her summer sailor uniform with a face like a glass mask that didn't seem to breathe and her eyes focused on the pages. I wonder if there's a reason she enjoys acquiring data through analog methods when she's more of a digital entity.

"..."

In any case, everybody had too much free time.

Today was a short day and school had officially been out before noon, so why were we all gathered in this place? That question was also directed at myself, but I had a legitimate reason. I have to drink one cup of Asahina's tea every day or I'll become a living corpse. Which is why I suffer from withdrawal on Saturdays and Sundays.

That was just a joke. That should go without saying, but I've learned since entering high school that some people have to be told that something's a joke. In fact, that's the only thing I've learned over the past few months so it has to be right. You should draw a clear line between jest and earnestness. Or else you'll run the risk of suffering an unpleasant experience.

The way I am now.

I opened my bag and took out the ham sandwich I'd redeemed from the school vendor to eat with my tea.

It was the time of year when everybody was counting down the days to summer vacation, so there was a reason all of us were lounging around in the club room like cats—or not. I'm fairly confident that there wasn't. After all, the SOS Brigade started up for no real reason, so there had never been an explanation for our presence here in the first place. I suppose that the lack of a reason would be the closest thing to a reason for any of this. Considering how stupid everything we do is, I'll have less of a headache if there isn't any meaning either. Since I won't have to do any thinking.

"I'll also take this chance to eat lunch."

After happily pouring herself some tea, Asahina took out an adorable-looking lunch box and sat down at the table across from me.

"Don't mind me. I ate in the cafeteria before coming here."

Koizumi spoke in a cheerful voice in response to a question nobody had asked. Nagato appeared to be more interested in reading than eating.

Asahina poked at her white rice with a smiley face drawn on it using the seasoning furikake.

"Where's Suzumiya? She's awfully late."

Why are you asking me? Maybe she's off somewhere trying to catch grasshoppers. Since it's summer.

Koizumi responded in my stead.

"I saw her in the cafeteria earlier. She had an admirable appetite. I can't even imagine how many ergs you would have if you were to convert the nutritional value of everything she ate."

And I don't feel like running the numbers. Hell, she can stay in the cafeteria until dinner if she wants.

"That won't happen. She seems to have an important announcement to make today."

I have no idea how you can look so cheerful. Her big announcements have never produced anything of value. Do you have less memory capacity than a five-and-a-quarter-inch floppy disk?

"Besides, how do you know about this?"

Koizumi feigned ignorance.

"Indeed, I wonder why. I could answer your question, but I believe that Suzumiya would prefer to tell you herself. It would be rather troublesome if I ruined her fun by telling you what she has to say. I'll keep my mouth shut."

"I didn't want to hear it myself."

"Is that so?"

"Yeah. Your tone basically told me that the idiot is up to another idiotic scheme. I don't know how many more minutes my peace of mind would have lasted, but it's obvious that the peace has been broken."

And as I was about to finish my remarks, the door slammed open.

"Okay, everybody's here, right?!"

Haruhi was standing there with eyes that shined like a spectroscope.

"We have an important meeting today. I'd planned on punishing anyone who showed up after I did by assigning them to be permanently It in a game of Kick the Can. It appears that you're all developing a sense of pride in being brigade members. That's a very good thing!"

I'm sure I don't need to tell you that I hadn't heard a thing about a meeting today.

"You sure took your time."

That was meant to be sarcastic.

"Okay? The trick to eating your fill at the cafeteria is to go right before they close. Then the cafeteria ladies will give you extra leftovers. But the timing is key. If you wait too long, everything could be sold out by the time you get there. Today was a lucky day."

"I see."

That was all I had to say in response to the worthless information presented with a boasting face, since I rarely ate in the cafeteria.

Haruhi sat down on the brigade chief's desk.

"Well, that doesn't really matter."

"You're the one who brought it up."

But Haruhi just ignored me and turned to Asahina, who was using her chopsticks in a proper manner.

"Mikuru, what do you think of when summer is mentioned?"

"Huh?"

Asahina covered her mouth as she chewed and swallowed the food that she'd made herself, apparently.

"Summer? Um, the Feast of Lanterns...I guess?"

A rather old-fashioned response, which made Haruhi blink a few times. "Feast of Lanterns? What's that? Sure you didn't mix that up with Halloween or something? That's not what I meant. There should be a word that instantly pops into your head the second you hear 'summer.'"

What's that?

Haruhi said in a matter-of-fact tone, "Summer vacation. Summer vacation. Shouldn't that be obvious?"

That's too obvious.

"And then, what does summer vacation make you think of?"

Haruhi rattled off the second question and looked at her watch as she made ticking sounds.

Asahina was drawn into Haruhi's flow as she frantically tried to come up with an answer.

"Um, well, th-the beach."

"Yep, yep. You're getting warmer now. And what does the beach make you think of?"

What is this? Some kind of word association game?

Asahina tilted the hairband on her head.

"Beach, beach, um...Ah, seafood?"

"Totally wrong. You're getting away from the subject of summer. What I'm trying to say is that you have to go on an overnight trip during summer vacation!"

I glared at Koizumi's increasingly irritating smile. This was the big announcement you were talking about?

"An overnight trip?"

I voiced my question and Haruhi nodded her head up and down.

"Yep, an overnight trip."

It makes sense for people in clubs to do an overnight trip or something during the summer, but what would be the purpose of our overnight trip? She couldn't be trying to get us to go into the mountains and capture some cryptid that's nowhere to be found.

I looked at Asahina, Koizumi, and Nagato, whose faces were surprised, smiling, and blank.

"An overnight trip, huh...For what purpose?"

"For the SOS Brigade," Haruhi replied.

"I mean, what are we going to do?"

"We're going on an overnight trip."

Hah? We're going on an overnight trip for the sake of going on an overnight trip. Isn't that like saying that a headache hurts, a tragedy is sad, or grilled fish is grilled?

"Who cares. In this case, the means and the ends are the same. Besides, isn't a headache supposed to hurt? It'd be weird if a headache felt good. So that statement's right."

Her mangling of the language made me wonder what dialect she was even using at this point, but in any case, the real problem here was the overnight trip thing.

"Where do you intend on going?"

"I intend on going to a remote island. In the middle of the ocean. One that requires a superlative adjective tacked on."

Well, I don't remember hearing anything about *Two Years' Vacation* being on the assigned reading list for summer vacation, so I wonder what she'd read to put that into her mind.

"I did a fair amount of thinking about potential destinations."

Haruhi was all smiles.

"I was fretting over whether to go to the mountains or the beach. At first, I thought that it'd be more convenient to go to the mountains, but you can only get trapped by a blizzard in a mountain retreat during winter."

You could just go to Greenland or something...I mean, I have to wonder why that's necessary.

"You want to go to a mountain retreat to be trapped in there?"

"That's right. Or else it wouldn't be any fun. But forget about the snowy mountains for now. We'll save that for the winter trip. We're going to the beach this summer! No, we're going to a remote island!"

I was thinking that she was awfully fixated on the remote island thing, but I didn't really feel like dissenting. Not that dissenting would have accomplished anything anyway. Besides, the beach is quite an attractive location this time of year. "So does this remote island in the middle of the ocean have a beach?"

"Of course! Isn't that right, Koizumi?"

"Yes, I believe so. Though it would be a completely natural beach without any lifeguards or carts selling roasted corn on the cob."

As Koizumi nodded, I shot him a questioning look. Why are you answering for her?

"That's because—" Koizumi said before he was interrupted by Haruhi.

"Koizumi is providing us with a place to stay during this trip!"

Haruhi had her hand stuck inside the desk as she scrounged around before pulling out what appeared to be an unmarked armband. She then wrote the words "Deputy Brigade Chief" on it in permanent marker.

"For this achievement, be happy, Koizumi, I'm promoting you two ranks and naming you the SOS Brigade deputy brigade chief!"

"It is an honor."

Koizumi respectfully accepted the armband before turning to me and winking. Just to be clear, I'm not jealous of you or anything. Why would anyone want a novelty item like that?

"And so, we'll be on an extravagant four-day three-night tour! Get psyched up and ready!"

Haruhi had a look on her face that suggested this discussion was over and we understood what was going on. Of course, we didn't.

"No, hold on a second."

I stepped up to speak on behalf of Asahina and Nagato.

"Where is this island you speak of? We've been invited? What's that? Why is Koizumi inviting us to this place?"

Koizumi, who had been defined by Haruhi as a mysterious transfer student, was obviously a shady character, but the stupid organization out there known as the "Agency" was even fishier. It could be some sort of trap in which our destination turned out to be a research facility where they would dissect Haruhi or Nagato or something.

"One of my distant relatives happens to be quite wealthy," Koizumi said as he flashed a harmless smile.

"He has enough money to buy a deserted island and build a villa there. In fact, he did just that. The manor was just completed a few days ago, but it's so far away that none of our acquaintances were inclined to make the trip. As he went down the list of friends and family for guests to invite, my turn eventually came around."

That's a suspicious-sounding island. I was reminded of the young adult book *Robinson Crusoe* that I'd read long ago.

"No, it was just a small deserted island to begin with. Summer vacation is coming up and it would be more fun if the members of the SOS Brigade went on a trip together. The owner of the villa is also looking forward to having us."

"There you have it!" said Haruhi.

She was smiling that peerless smile which tended to show up when she was making trouble for us.

"It's a remote island! And a manor! A rare situation. It's like, who's supposed to go if we're not going? This is an ideal stage for the SOS Brigade's summer camp!"

"Why?" I asked. "What does a manor on a remote island have to do with those searches for the supernatural you love?"

But Haruhi was already in her own little world.

"A remote island in the middle of the ocean, surrounded by water on every side! With a manor! Koizumi, your relative knows what he's doing! Yep, I have a feeling I'll hit it off with him."

Any person that can hit it off with Haruhi is guaranteed to be a deviant with no exceptions, so the master of that manor must be a deviant. If he hits it off with her, at least.

I had no idea if Nagato was even listening to Haruhi's little speech, but Asahina was in a slight daze and she'd stopped eating her lunch.

"Don't worry, Mikuru. You'll get to eat all the fresh seafood you want. Isn't that right?"

"It'll be arranged," said Koizumi.

"There you have it."

Haruhi took another unmarked armband out of the desk. How many extras do you have?

"We're off to the remote island! I'm certain that something fun awaits us there. My role has already been decided!"

She was writing on the armband with a permanent marker as she spoke. Her wild handwriting spelled out, as far as I could tell, the words "great detective."

"Why don't you tell me what you're plotting?"

"Nothing at all," Koizumi said in casual denial.

Once Haruhi had been satisfied by delivering her important announcement, she called it a day and left. Asahina and Nagato also left the club room to head home. Only Koizumi and I remained.

Koizumi ran his hands through his hair.

"I'm telling the truth. Suzumiya would still have planned a trip of some sort if I hadn't spoken up. Since summer vacation feels short yet long. Would you have preferred hunting for *tsuchinoko* instead of going to the beach or the mountains?"

"What's this *tsuchinoko* thing—no, never mind. Don't explain what a *tsuchinoko* is. I can figure it out for myself."

"Three days ago, I ran into Suzumiya at the bookstore by the station. She was staring intently at a map of Japan. She was also looking through an occult magazine that was doing a special on cryptids."

A trip to search for cryptids, huh? The thought is enough to send shivers up my spine. We're talking about Haruhi here. I'm scared that we might actually find something.

"Right? It appears that Suzumiya intends to go catch something. I have a hunch that the Hiba Mountains are at the top of her list of potential destinations. In which case, you could say that sunbathing on the beach would please the greatest number of people possible. And I happened to have an appropriate destination."

No idea how you happened to conveniently have such a perfect destination ready. Well, if you compare hiking through the mountains under the blazing sun with watching the female brigade members wearing swimsuits on the beach, it's like comparing hell to a utopia.

"The deciding factor was the fact that this was a privately owned deserted island. She mentioned something about a closed circle."

Naturally, I had to ask. It's a good idea to ask questions when you don't know something.

"What's a closed circle?"

Koizumi had a smile on his face that was completely free of sarcasm. I could plainly see that if someone felt he was being sarcastic, they were blind.

"This may only serve as a loose explanation."

Koizumi paused for a moment without losing his smile.

"I suppose that you could say it's closed space."

I had no idea how the expression on my face could be considered funny, but Koizumi chuckled.

"That was a joke. 'Closed circle' is a mystery term. It refers to a situation where contact with the outside world has been severed."

Speak in a language I can understand.

"It's one of the common settings the characters of classic mystery stories find themselves in. Allow me to offer an example. For instance, say that we were to go on a skiing trip in the middle of winter."

That reminds me that Haruhi said something about snowy mountains.

"So we've managed to find lodging on said snowy mountain, but then we run into a record blizzard."

If you're going to a place like that, you should check the weather forecast first.

"Well, now we're in trouble. Storm force winds and snow accumulation prevent us from descending the mountain. And nobody else can make their way to the mountain retreat."

So deal with it.

"It's called a closed circle because nothing can be done. And then something happens under these circumstances. The most popular incident would be a murder. This is where the setting is truly allowed to shine. The culprit and other characters are unable to escape the building. At the same time, there won't be any new characters coming from the outside. It would be especially unreasonable for the police to show up, since it wouldn't be very interesting to use a forensic investigation to identify the culprit."

As always, I have no idea what this guy is talking about.

"Oh, excuse me. To summarize, Suzumiya's desired theme is to become involved in a situation out of a mystery."

"And that requires an island?"

"Yes, a remote island. She may be envisioning a serial murder case where we're trapped on the island and nobody can escape. As far as closed circles go, a mountain retreat during a blizzard and a remote island are exceptional settings able to cancel out any potential intervention by authorities."

"I can't say I'm too thrilled about how you seem to be enjoying yourself."

Haruhi's tendency to run wild wasn't limited to summertime or anything, but there wasn't any need for you to cheer her on. And it's not like I'm sulking because I wasn't named deputy brigade chief.

"To be honest, I also happen to enjoy such situations."

I have no intention of criticizing somebody else's tastes, but let me say one thing. I don't like this at all.

However, Koizumi paid no heed to my tastes and continued in a tone that sounded like he was reading an essay.

"Let us consider famous detectives. It would be rare for people who live ordinary lives to become involved in bizarre murder cases, correct?"

"Well, yeah."

"However, the great detectives found in literary work are somehow caught up in one baffling case after the next. Why do you think that is?"

"There wouldn't be a story otherwise."

"Exactly. You are absolutely correct. Such incidents are fiction. They only exist in the unrealistic world of storytelling. However, it would be rather blunt to say such metafictional things. After all, Suzumiya fully intends to cast herself into the world of fiction."

Now that you mention it, that was the reason she made the SOS Brigade, wasn't it?

"One must travel to the appropriate locations to encounter such unrealistic and mysterious happenings. For that is how the great detectives of literature become involved in cases. You could say that it is necessary to become a relevant party in the case. Cases won't come flying in by themselves unless there's a relative that's a police bigwig or the main character is a police officer or we're dealing with a running series that's gone through multiple books."

I see. I knew that Nagato was a science fiction fan, but I had no idea that you were a mystery lover. And I'm guessing that Haruhi loves both.

"For an amateur to play the role of detective, that person must first be unintentionally dragged into an incident that has occurred in the vicinity and the case must be solved swiftly."

"There's no way that something is just going to happen around you so conveniently."

Koizumi nodded.

"Yes. Reality is unlike the world of fiction. There is a minimal chance of an interesting sealed room murder occurring in our school. In that case, we should go to a place with a higher likelihood of something occurring; at least, that must be what Suzumiya is thinking."

I was reminded of the phrase "the tail wagging the dog."

"That would be the location of this trip, the remote island. I do not know the reason, but such a place is generally accepted by society as an appropriate stage for a murder."

What society are you talking about? That's one narrow-minded society.

"Putting it another way, you could say that strange happenings occur wherever a great detective goes. Humans labeled as great detectives possess the supernatural ability to attract trouble instead of merely happening upon it. That is the only explanation I can think of. Cases do not lead to the appearance of detectives. Rather, the presence of a detective leads to the birth of a case."

I gave Koizumi a look as though I had just accidentally stepped on a sea slug.

"Are you sane?"

"I believe that my actions can always be considered within the realm of sanity. Everything I've said concerning detectives, closed circles, and the ilk has not been a result of my own deliberation. Rather, I was merely tracing Suzumiya's pattern of thinking. In other words, the simple way to put it would be that she wants to be a detective. That is the purpose of this trip."

How is she going to become a great detective? I suppose she could fake a whole case by playing both the culprit and the detective.

"Nevertheless, I believed this to be a better alternative to hunting for *tsuchinoko*. All I did was mention to Suzumiya that an acquaintance had built a villa on an island and was looking for guests. I personally do not expect any murders to occur, obviously."

Koizumi's cheerful smile pisses me off every time I see it. And the way he shrugs too.

"I merely offered Suzumiya an opportunity for a little entertainment. Or else, who knows what she might come up with to deal with her boredom? In which case, preparing a stage beforehand allows for us to prepare a number of safety measures."

"Us, huh?"

Upon seeing my discouraged look, Koizumi attempted to smooth things over.

"The 'Agency' has nothing to do with this affair. Though I filed a report to be safe. I may be an esper, but at my core, I am a high school student. What's wrong with going on a trip? What you would expect in the life of a high school student. A trip with some close friends would be an exciting occasion, correct?"

Only if the reason Haruhi's excited is because she's going on a trip. Maybe if we were going to a normal hot spring or a beach on the mainland, but our destination is a remote island, you know? We're talking about Haruhi here. She might call in a couple hurricanes…

…Well, I'm pretty sure that she isn't crazy enough to cause a murder. Or else we'd have a pile of dead bodies in North High by now. Anyway, I had a feeling there was something else important as I lost myself in deep thought.

A four-day three-night trip to the beach in the summer. With beaches of white sand and a blazing sun over our heads. In that case, I'm willing to put up with this wretched heat a little longer. Slave away, Mr. Sun.

Okay, I need to start preparing to drool over the sight of Asahina in a swimsuit.

In a generous gesture, the lodging would be provided free of charge. No expenses for food either. All we had to pay was the price of the ferry trip in both directions.

And so, we were now on the boarding platform in the harbor eagerly awaiting the boarding time for the ferry.

Haruhi must have been in a big rush to go on a trip. The first semester had ended yesterday, which meant that today was the first day of summer vacation. Koizumi and his people told us that we could go whenever we wanted, but the fact that Haruhi wanted to leave the second vacation started says a lot about her impatient personality, I'd say. I'd been planning on spending a few days without having to see Haruhi's face, but the person known as Haruhi Suzumiya wouldn't allow that to happen. You could call that the purpose of her existence.

"I haven't been on a ferry in a long time."

With a visor on her head at a slanted angle, Haruhi stood at the edge of the wharf and gazed at the lead-colored sea. The sticky sea breeze sent her black hair fluttering as we lined up at the front of the boarding dock.

"This is such a big boat. I wonder how it manages to stay afloat."

Asahina held a bag with both arms as she admired the body of the boat. She looked lovely in a white summer dress with a straw hat over her head. The laces of the hat were even tied under her chin in a manner you would expect from Asahina. Her childlike eyes were shining as she gazed at the old ferry as though it were an ancient artifact that had been dug out of some ruins. Maybe the boats don't float on water in her time.

"..."

Nagato stood behind her in a daze as she stared at the name of the corporation written on the side of the boat. Oddly enough, Nagato wasn't wearing her school uniform. She was wearing a checkered sleeveless affair and holding a yellow-green umbrella, which provided some shade. She had the aura of a sickly girl who'd just been released from the hospital. I wanted to go buy an instant camera and take a picture. I could probably sell it to Taniguchi or something for a good price.

"It appears we've been blessed with clear weather. You could say that the conditions are perfect for sailing. Though we'll be in the second-class cabin," said Koizumi.

"That's fair enough."

We were in a large room without anything that could be considered a partition. The voyage would take a number of hours, but we'd have to live another ten years or so before we could deserve private cabins. After all, we're just a bunch of high schoolers going on a trip.

The real problem here would be that this couldn't be considered a club trip. You can't call a trip for the sake of going on a trip a meaningful activity. Besides, aren't normal club trips supposed to have an advisor supervising? The SOS Brigade doesn't even have one. We're a club that hasn't been approved by the school so I'd be surprised if we did have one. At North High, you can't even be considered a student association if you don't have an advisor, and I have a hunch that even if we managed to find a teacher willing to be the SOS Brigade's advisor, Haruhi would deem it unnecessary. If she actually thought that we needed one, she would have kidnapped someone by now. The way she did us.

I yawned as Asahina walked over to me. Her wide eyes were even wider than usual.

"How does such a big boat stay afloat?"

How? What reason could there be besides buoyancy? Do they not have science classes in Asahina's time?

"Ah, I see. Buoyancy. Th-That's right. I get it. This would be what they mean by being unable to see the forest for the trees."

I have no idea why she was so excited, but Asahina was nodding to herself with a look on her face like she was about to run out of the bath screaming eureka.

I decided to try asking a question. It couldn't hurt to ask a question.

"Say, Asahina. Do boats in the future use some kind of ground-breaking method to float?"

"Hmm. Do you think I'm allowed to tell you?" she responded with a question.

I shook my head. I seriously doubt it. I switched to a different line of questioning.

"Are there oceans in the future?"

Asahina tugged slightly at the brim of her hat.

"Yes, there are. There are oceans."

"That's good to hear."

I don't know if she's from the near future or the distant future, but I'm glad that Earth hasn't turned into a complete desert. Though I have to hope that the composition of seawater has improved by then.

And right when I was getting enthusiastic about prying some beneficial information out of the time traveler...

"Kyon! Mikuru! What are you doing? It's time!" Haruhi yelled to let us know that it was time to board the ship.

By the way, I had showed up after the meeting time today. When I left the house this morning, I'd picked up my duffel bag to find it oddly heavy. Suspicious, I opened it up to find that my clothes and toiletries had been replaced by my little sister. Last night,

I'd accidentally let it slip that I'd be going on a trip with Haruhi and the others, which led to my sister screaming that she wanted to go too. It'd taken two whole hours to get her calmed down, but I guess she'd come up with a plan to smuggle herself along. I dumped my sister out of the bag and asked her where she'd hidden my stuff. Once she took the fifth, I wasted a good deal of time trying to coax and force the information out of her. I'm not going to buy you any souvenirs. Since that money's being used to buy the SOS Brigade box lunches on the ferry.

The members of the SOS Brigade were gathered in a corner of the second-class drawing room as we chatted while eating the box lunches I'd been forced to buy. Though Haruhi and Koizumi did most of the talking.

"How much longer until we get there?"

"The trip by ferry takes approximately six hours. I have arranged for an acquaintance to be waiting at our port of arrival. From there, we'll be taking a private cruiser for approximately thirty minutes. The remote island and towering manor await us at the voyage's end. I've never been there before so I can't tell you how the location is."

"I'm sure it's a strange-looking building. Do you know the name of the person who designed it?" Haruhi asked as she practically jumped up and down with excitement.

"I didn't inquire about that. I believe a somewhat famous architect was commissioned for the job."

"I can't wait to see it."

"I hope it meets your expectations, but I didn't see the place beforehand so I wouldn't know. However, it was built by a person who wanted to erect a private villa on a deserted island, so I would assume that it's special in some way. At least, I hope so."

Koizumi might hope so, but I sure don't. Let us picture a design that would satisfy Haruhi's expectations. It would probably look like something designed by an inebriated Gaudi who had just pulled three straight all-nighters. I sure don't want to stay in such a freaky-looking mansion. I'd prefer to stay in an ordinary inn. A traditional Japanese-styled one that serves roasted seaweed and raw eggs for breakfast. And if it was a special house, could Haruhi kill someone and make a case happen?

"Island! Manor! You couldn't find a better location for the SOS Brigade's summer camp. This is the perfect way to start off our summer vacation."

As Haruhi celebrated, the rest of the brigade members stood around her in silence.

As there was nothing to do besides be rocked by the waves, we went with Koizumi's idea of playing Old Maid. Koizumi, the loser, was forced to buy juice for the rest of us, which we drank in silence.

I couldn't help feeling uneasy about our destination being a remote island with a manor and all the other obscure details. It appeared that Asahina shared the sentiment.

Haruhi finished her juice in two gulps.

"Mikuru, you look pale. Are you seasick?"

"No...Um...Ah, that may be it," Asahina responded before Haruhi spoke again.

"That's no good. You should go outside. You'll feel much better once you're out on the deck and breathing in the sea air. Come on, let's go."

And with that, she took Asahina's hand and grinned.

"There's no need to worry. I won't push you into the ocean. Hmm...that doesn't sound bad. The sudden disappearance of a female passenger on a boat."

"Eek."

Asahina froze and Haruhi slapped her shoulder.

"I'm joking. Just kidding. That wouldn't be any fun at all. This boat has to run into an iceberg or be attacked by a monster squid before I could classify it as a serious incident."

I'll check where the lifeboats are located later. I doubt any icebergs are floating around the coastal waters of Japan in the middle of summer, but I could see some unknown water-dwelling creature popping out of nowhere. I shot a look in an attempt to tell them to take out the monster if it showed up, but Koizumi merely smiled at me and Nagato continued staring at the wall.

Haruhi was still talking by herself.

"Incidents are supposed to happen on remote islands! Koizumi, I won't be disappointed, right?!"

"There are no significant events scheduled," Koizumi responded mildly. "I also wish for this to be a pleasant trip."

Koizumi smiled the ambiguous smile typical of people saying insincere things. Though I suppose that was the usual expression on his face, I stared at the stupid esper in an attempt to break through that smiling mask, but I soon gave up. His smile, just like Nagato's poker face, reveals no information. Seriously, can't you people show some human emotion? Just not as much as Haruhi, please.

Haruhi hummed a random tune as she led Asahina outside the cabin. Asahina kept looking back at me like she was hoping I'd come along, but that could have just been a wrong assumption on my part, and I didn't want to ruin Haruhi's mood by tagging along so I didn't.

I'm pretty sure that Haruhi would still save Asahina from falling into the ocean. I looked up at the ceiling and prayed that was true before lying down sideways with my bag as a pillow. I'd woken up early this morning, so I figured I'd get some sleep for now.

I had a feeling that my dream had involved something of a fantasy nature, but before I could remember any details I was slapped awake and receiving a directive transmission from Haruhi.

"What are you sleeping for, stupid? Get up already. Do you even intend to be serious about this trip? How much use will you be if you're like this on the boat ride there?"

It appeared that we had arrived at the stopover island while I was asleep, and I felt as though I'd lost something irreplaceable.

"The first step is key. You don't have the mentality to enjoy things. Look at how those eyes are shining with excitement about this trip."

Haruhi was pointing at the three servants disembarking from the ship with their belongings.

One of them was a smiling boy.

"Now, now, Suzumiya. I'm sure that he's saving his energy for the rest of the trip. He probably intends to stay awake the whole night to come up with ways to entertain us."

As I listened to Koizumi's unneeded follow-up, I searched Nagato's automaton-like face for these so-called shining eyes and I also glanced at Asahina's eyes, which resembled those of a small animal.

"We're already there?" I muttered.

A multihour trip. With the members of the SOS Brigade. No, I could care less about the other people. I had given into my desire to sleep and killed an opportunity to spend quality time with Asahina inside the cabin.

Whoa. I'd already jinxed myself. Should I really be spending my summer vacation like this? The only memory I'd have of this day so far would be playing Old Maid. What happened to the two of us chatting while standing in the cool sea breeze?

I felt like grabbing the me who had fallen asleep a few hours ago and kicking him a few times.

Click.

I was blinded by a sudden flash.

I turned toward the source of the sound to find Asahina holding a camera. The child-faced angel had a lovely smile.

"He-he. I took a picture of you waking up."

She looked like a preschooler who had just pulled off a prank.

"I also took a picture of you while you were sleeping. Did you sleep well?"

I instantly cheered up. I wonder why Asahina was secretly taking pictures of me. Could it be that she actually wanted a picture of me? One to slip into a cute frame and place by her bed for her to say good night to every evening? That sounds nice. Let's go with that.

Man, if you'd told me that you wanted a picture, I'd have been more than happy to give you as many as you wanted. I'll even show you my albums once I figure out where they're tucked away.

However, I was about to voice that sentiment when Asahina handed the instant camera to Haruhi.

"Kyon, what are you grinning about? It makes you look like an idiot so you'd better stop."

As she put the camera in her bag, Haruhi had a look on her face like she was planning on selling exclusive photos of an accident scene to some newspaper.

"Mikuru is serving as the temporary SOS Brigade photographer for this trip. We aren't taking pictures for fun. These will serve as important materials for leaving a record of our club activities for posterity. But we can't allow this girl to take pictures of whatever she wants, so I'll be instructing her."

And how are pictures of me sleeping and waking up considered important materials?

"The pictures of you sleeping with a stupid face completely free of any concern about this trip will serve as a warning to future generations! Understood? An underling snoring away when the chief is awake goes against morals, natural order, and brigade code!"

I couldn't tell if Haruhi was angry or laughing as she glared at me. It appeared that it would be futile to ask when a brigade code had been made up. It probably wasn't anything in writing, so I'll just let it slide like an Egyptian.

"Got it. So if I don't want my face drawn on, I can't go to sleep before you do? But in that case, if I wake up before you, I should be allowed to draw a mustache on your face."

"What's that? You want to do something that childish? Just so you know, my senses are so sharp that I even hit back in my sleep. And a brigade member committing such offenses against the brigade chief would lead to heads rolling."

You know, Haruhi, the majority of modern countries don't behead people anymore. What do you have to say about that?

"Why do I have to comment on the penal practices of other countries? The trouble isn't going to happen in a foreign country. We'll find it on the mysterious island we're headed for!"

As I adjusted my bag, I prayed that her "find" wasn't going to turn into a "make."

The boat rocked back and forth. It appeared that we were preparing to dock at the wharf. The other passengers were headed toward the vicinity of the exit.

"A mysterious island, huh..."

Are we headed for Panorama Island or something? I just hope that the island won't suddenly rise out of the water or start moving.

"It'll be fine."

Koizumi nodded, appearing to have read my mind.

"It's simply a small, removed island with nothing unusual about it. You won't find any monsters or crazy scientists there. You have my word."

This guy's word hasn't been very dependable. I silently looked at Nagato's pale face.

"…"

Nagato silently looked back. I suppose that she can slay monsters if it comes to that. I'm counting on you, E.T.

The boat rocked again.

"Eek."

Asahina lost her balance, but Nagato was there to silently hold her up.

We disembarked from the ferry to find a butler and maid waiting for us.

"Hello, Arakawa. It's been quite some time."

Koizumi cheerfully waved one hand.

"And you, Mori. Thank you for coming to meet us. Sorry to trouble you."

Koizumi then turned back to us, standing dumbfounded, and spread his arms in an exaggerated motion like a stage actor focused on making sure the people in the nosebleed section can see what he's doing. His usual smile was four times wider than usual.

"Allow me to introduce you. These are the two people who manage the manor we will be staying in, Arakawa and Mori. Their respective positions are butler and maid. Ah, I suppose you can see that."

No kidding. I took another look at the two peculiarities who remained bowed. You couldn't help staring at them.

"We have been awaiting your arrival. I am the butler, Arakawa."

An old tuxedo-clad gentleman with white hair, eyebrows, and mustache greeted us and bowed again.

"My name is Sonoh Mori. I serve as the maid. It is a pleasure to meet you."

The woman next to him lowered her head at the same angle. Then they both straightened together with timing so exact you had to wonder how many times they'd practiced this.

Arakawa appeared to be fairly old, but it was hard to judge what his actual age was. It was also difficult to gauge the age of the maid, Sonoh Mori. She appeared young enough to be our age, but that could have been a product of makeup, or she simply had a baby face.

"A butler and maid?" Haruhi murmured in surprise.

I felt the same way. I had no idea that such professions actually existed in Japan. I figured that the concept had become a relic of the past.

I see. The two people standing behind Koizumi definitely looked like a butler and maid. At the very least, if they introduced themselves as such, you'd have no choice but to nod and agree. Especially the maid, Mori, I believe. She looked like a maid in every possible way. Because she was wearing a maid outfit. I've spent every day looking at Asahina wearing her maid outfit in the literary club room, so I know what I'm talking about. And the outfits worn by Arakawa and Mori hadn't come from Haruhi's need for pointless costume play. That was the necessary dress for their actual professions.

"Wah..."

In a daze Asahina gazed at the two of them—Mori, to be specific—with a surprised look on her face. Though I suppose it was half surprise and around 30 percent confusion. Who knows what the remaining 20 percent would be considered? There may have been some envy mixed in. Perhaps she'd actually developed a desire to become a real maid after Haruhi kept forcing it on her.

As for Nagato, she hadn't made a single comment and her face hadn't even twitched. She stared at the two professionals who made up our reception with eyes like obsidian barbs from the Old Stone Age.

"Now then, everyone," Arakawa called to us in a rich tenor like that of an opera singer.

"I have prepared a boat over here. It will be a half-hour voyage by boat to reach my master's island. I hope you can forgive the inconvenience of being located on a remote island."

He and Mori bowed again. I was feeling pretty uncomfortable. I wanted to tell them we didn't warrant such courteous treatment. Or is Koizumi the son of some rich family? I figured that his specialty was being an irregular esper, but maybe his family was rich enough for him to be called "young master" at home.

"It's totally not a problem!"

Haruhi shouted in a voice that instantly scattered all the question marks in my mind. I turned to find that Haruhi had a smile on her face like a bogus movie producer who had just squeezed a large sum of money from a stupid sponsor.

"That's what makes it a remote island! Half an hour is nothing. You can take as many hours as you want. After all, I'm looking for a remote island in the middle of the ocean. Kyon, Mikuru, you should be happier about this. We have a remote island with a manor and there's even a suspicious-looking butler and maid. You could search all of Japan and only find two islands like this!"

There isn't a second one.

"W-Wow. So amazing...I can't wait."

Moving past Asahina's failed attempt to sound excited, Haruhi is taking rude to a new level when she's calling people "suspicious-looking" to their face.

Well, this whole situation is pretty shady, and quite frankly, the SOS Brigade isn't any less suspicious so we aren't really in a position to talk about others, but I don't see why events had to play out in a way that left Haruhi on a perpetual high.

As I watched Koizumi chat with Arakawa the butler and Mori the maid standing by with her hands clasped, I had an urge to look out into the sea. Calm waves and clear skies. No sign of an impending hurricane so far.

Will we ever step foot on the mainland again?

Nagato's cool poker face looked very reassuring. Pathetic, huh?

Arakawa and Mori led us to a small wharf near the ferry dock. I had been expecting a pop-pop boat, but instead, a private cruiser out of a picture of the Mediterranean was rocking in the waves. It looked so fancy I didn't even want to ask how much it cost, though I could totally picture catching a swordfish while riding this thing.

I was too careless. While ignoring Haruhi, who just jumped onboard herself, Koizumi helped the timid Asahina and indifferent Nagato onto the ship. That should have been my job, but groaning about it failed to turn the clock back.

We were led into the cabin, and before I could even start wondering why such a fancy Western-style reception room was inside a boat, the cruiser gently set off. So it appears that butlers have boat permits these days since Arakawa was the one at the helm.

Incidentally, Sonoh Mori was sitting across from me with a gentle smile, like she was a fixture on this ship. Her maid attire was chic and fundamentally sound. I had a feeling that it wasn't as stimulating as the outfit Haruhi made Asahina wear in the club room, but since I wasn't particularly well versed in the world of maid outfits, I wasn't really sure.

I wasn't the only person feeling uneasy, as Asahina had been glancing over at the maid's garb. Maybe she wants to ask about the experiences of a real maid on the job as a reference for how to behave in the club room. She tends to be serious about the oddest things.

Nagato was sitting rigidly in a forward position while Koizumi remained composed with the usual smile on his face.

"This is a nice boat. Perhaps we should add fishing to the schedule?" he proposed to no one in particular.

And as for Haruhi—

"So what do you call that building?"

"What do you mean?"

"Does it have a name along the lines of House of Black Death, Crooked Mansion, Lolac Villa, or Koketsu Castle?"

"No, not particularly."

"Are there any terrifying stories about strange hidden mechanisms or the architect dying an unnatural death or a room where any person who spends a night will die?"

"None that I am aware of."

"In that case, does the master of the manor wear a mask or hear the voices of his three sisters inside his head, and then there were none?"

"Not at all."

The butler chimed in. "Nothing like that at the moment."

"Then there's a pretty high chance that something will happen in the future, right?"

"That may be the case."

This butler is just telling her what she wants to hear.

As soon as the boat had set off, Haruhi had climbed up to the cockpit of the boat and engaged in the above conversation with Arakawa. From what I could hear of their conversation over the sound of the engine and splashing waves, it seemed that Haruhi was expecting way too much from this manor on a remote island. In any case, why does she insist that the island have a bizarre nature simply because it's removed from land? Can't she be satisfied by taking a swim, eating good food, lying around, and strengthening our friendship before going home happily? I sincerely hope she can.

Though it may already be too late.

The appearance of a butler and maid had been more unexpected than a blue shark showing up in a public pool, so at this point, I wouldn't really have been surprised if the master of the manor wore a mask or there were other guests who behaved in a suspicious manner. Damn Koizumi. What other tricks do you have up your sleeve?

"Wow! I can see it! Is that the villa?"

"That would be the manor," Haruhi's conspicuously loud and lovely voice boomed through the air, stabbing my heart like thunder.

The villa or whatever actually looked pretty normal.

The sun was on its way down, but there was still time before dusk. As sunlight fell upon the manor, I almost thought that it was shining. After all, I'd never dreamed that I'd ever set foot in something like a villa.

The building enshrined atop a vertical cliff didn't appear any different from what you'd expect from a manor constructed as a rich person's summer getaway, though it didn't appear to be based on an old castle from Europe, it wasn't a brick-colored house entwined in vines, it didn't have any strange towers attached, and it didn't seem to conceal any funny gimmicks like the ones you'd find in a ninja house.

As expected, Haruhi had a look on her face like someone served onion rings after expecting pork chops as she gazed at the villa (manor, according to Haruhi) in the distance.

"Hmm. This isn't quite what I was expecting. I believe that the

appearance is a critical element. I wonder if the architect refer-
enced older documents in the process."

I stood next to Haruhi on the deck as I took in the scenery. I'd
been dragged out of the cabin by her.

"What do you think about that, Kyon? The building looks surprisingly normal for something on a remote island. Don't you
find that a waste?"

I sure do. Why do you need to build a villa in this place? It's an
hour-long round trip by private cruiser just to go to the convenience
store. Where do you go if you're feeling hungry in the middle of the
night? And I doubt there are any vending machines around.

"I'm talking about the atmosphere. I'd been convinced that the
place would be more eerie-looking. This is what I'd expect from
a quiet tourist destination. We aren't here to have fun at a rich
friend's summer home."

I brushed away the strands of Haruhi's hair that were blowing
in the wind and prickling my face.

"That's right. This is supposed to be a summer camp. What
kind of activities do you have planned? Are we going to pretend to be adventurers? Simulate what would happen if we were
stranded on a deserted island?"

"Ah, that's a good idea. I'll add island exploration to the agenda.
Maybe we can discover a new species."

Not good. I just said something to make Haruhi's eyes shine
brighter. Please don't let anything unneeded show up, island.

I directed that thought in the direction of the island covered
in green.

"It appears that the islands in this area were formed long ago
when underwater volcanoes erupted," Koizumi said as he slowly
walked out.

"New species aside, there is a possibility that we may discover
shards of earthenware left by ancient tribes. Or traces left by

the proto-Japanese during their voyage across the sea. Isn't it romantic?"

I don't see any connection between the romance of archaeology and this newly built villa, but I definitely don't want to go around looking for *tsuchinoko* or digging holes. We can split into two groups. Haruhi and Koizumi can explore the island while Asahina, Nagato, and I play on the beach. Nice idea.

"Oh? I see somebody over there."

Haruhi pointed to a small wharf that I would expect to have been newly constructed. Apparently, the harbor was specifically meant for the cruiser as there were no other boats in sight. A single figure stood at the end of the breakwater-like structure and waved to us. It appeared to be a man.

Haruhi reflexively waved back.

"Koizumi, is that man the master of the manor? He looks awfully young."

Koizumi was also waving.

"No, that isn't him. He's also an invited guest. The younger brother of the owner of the manor. I've met him once before."

"Koizumi," I interjected. "Tell us these things earlier. This is the first I've heard about any other guests."

"I just found out about him now." Koizumi casually shrugged me off. "But there is no need to worry. He is a very nice person. Of course, the same can be said of the owner of the manor, Keiichi Tamaru."

I'd heard that this Keiichi Tamaru was crazy enough to build a villa in this remote place as a summer residence. He was a distant relative of Koizumi's, like his mother's cousin or something along those lines. I'm not really sure, but he'd hit the jackpot in biotechnology and was now living a very comfortable life. He probably had more money than he knew how to spend. Or else I wouldn't be able to understand why he built this thing.

The cruiser slowed down as it approached the harbor. We were close enough for me to make out the features of the man standing on the dock. He was dressed in youthful attire and looked to be in his twenties. This was Keiichi Tamaru's younger brother, apparently.

Arakawa was the butler and Sonoh Mori was the maid.

That left the star, the master of the manor, Keiichi Tamaru.

Was it safe to assume that we'd covered all the characters who would be showing up?

Thinking back, I'd spent hours on shaking boats today...Which was why I felt like the ground was shaking right now.

Once we'd disembarked from the cruiser and stepped onto firm land, the young man greeted us with a cheerful smile.

"Hey, Itsuki. It's been a long time."

"Indeed, Yutaka. Thank you for coming to meet us."

Koizumi nodded before introducing us.

"These are the people who look after me at school."

Not that I remember ever looking after him. Koizumi began working down the line, point to each of us one by one.

"This lovely young lady is Haruhi Suzumiya. A rare friend. She always acts in an open and natural manner, something I would love to learn to do."

What kind of introduction is that? I can feel sweat dripping down my back. You too, Haruhi. Come on. Why are you pretending to act all refined and polite? Did your brain get jumbled up from being seasick?

However, Haruhi smiled a blindingly brilliant smile.

"I am Suzumiya. Koizumi is an invaluable member of my brigade...I mean, student association. Koizumi was the one who invited us to this island. He always serves as a reliable deputy brigade...I mean, vice president. Ahem."

Koizumi ignored the frosty look I was sending him and continued with his introductions.

"This is Mikuru Asahina. As you can see, she's an upperclassman who's considered the lovely and beautiful idol of our school. Her smile could bring world peace to fruition."

There's one.

"This is Yuki Nagato. She's a veritable gold mine of information that can't be found in our textbooks. She's soft-spoken, but that could be considered as one of her endearing qualities."

And there was another profile that set my teeth on edge. Naturally, I was also given introductions riddled with embellished compliments like something you'd find in a personal ad, but I'll skip over that part.

Yutaka flashed a brilliant smile befitting a relative of Koizumi's.

"Welcome. I'm Yutaka Tamaru. I've been hired to help out at my brother's company. I've heard much about you all from Itsuki. I was worried when he suddenly had to transfer, but I'm glad he's made such wonderful friends."

"Everybody," Arakawa's melodiously gruff voice came from behind.

I turned to find the butler, carrying a fairly large burden, and Sonoh Mori getting off the boat.

"We're exposed to the sun here. Why don't we move to the villa?"

Yutaka nodded in response to Arakawa's suggestion.

"You have a point. My brother's also waiting. Let's take the luggage with us. I'll help out."

"We should be fine. Please assist Arakawa and Mori. It appears that they bought a large amount of groceries on the main island."

Yutaka returned Koizumi's smile with a smile of his own.

"That gives me something to look forward to."

And once the harmless chitchat was over with, we followed Koizumi toward the villa on the cliff.

Looking back, this was when I started to have a funny feeling about things.

Though as they say, hindsight is 20/20.

To reach the villa we climbed our way up a staircase resembling the one leading up to the eighth station on Mount Fuji. My condolences to Haruhi, but this place was definitely a villa and not a manor or mansion.

The white structure was three stories high yet it felt flat, probably because it took up a ridiculous amount of space. I almost wanted to count how many rooms there were. You could probably have housed two whole soccer teams in this place. A portion of the thick foliage had been cleared off to build the villa, but how had they managed to ship all the necessary construction materials here? That would have required a fairly large-scale heliborne operation. I don't understand rich people.

"This way, please."

Koizumi led us to the entrance like a butler-in-training. Everybody lined up in a row. We were finally about to meet the master of the manor. A nerve-wracking moment.

Haruhi was standing in front of the rest of us like a horse racing ahead of the herd. I could see that she was having a hard time containing her anticipation as she licked her lips. Asahina was fussing over her hair in an adorable fashion so she would make a good first impression. Nagato, as usual, stood completely still without any visible signs of sweating, like one of those lucky cat statues.

Koizumi looked back at us before smiling thinly and coolly pressing the button on the intercom next to the door.

Someone answered and Koizumi responded with a greeting. After we waited for about half a minute, the door slowly opened.

Needless to say, the man standing in front of us wasn't wearing an iron mask or a ski mask with sunglasses and he didn't suddenly attack us or yell obscure gibberish to confuse us. He was just a normal-looking middle-aged man.

"Welcome."

The man who was supposed to be Keiichi Tamaru was allegedly a self-made millionaire, but he looked to be a normal old guy in a golf shirt and cargo pants as he beckoned us over with one hand.

"We've been waiting for you, Itsuki. And your friends as well. Quite frankly, this is a terribly boring place. You'll be sick of it by the third day. The only other person who accepted my invitation was Yutaka. Oh!"

Keiichi's gaze glided past me to reach Asahina, Haruhi, and Nagato in that order.

"Well, well. You have some lovely friends, Itsuki, I see. They're just as beautiful as I've heard. They'll add some color to this dreary island. That's just splendid."

Haruhi smiled, Asahina bowed, and Nagato stood still. The three of them reacted in different ways as they looked at Keiichi offering a warm welcome, the way you would look at a music teacher showing up for history class. Eventually, Haruhi stepped forward.

"I would like to express my sincere gratitude for your invitation today. I truly appreciate the opportunity to stay in such a wonderful mansion. On behalf of everyone here, I offer our thanks."

She sounded like she was reading off a script an octave higher than her normal voice. Does she intend to keep pretending to be a nice girl for the rest of the trip? She should drop that flimsy act before she lets her true nature slip.

Keiichi Tamaru apparently agreed.

"Are you Suzumiya? My, you sure are different from what I've heard. According to Itsuki, you were... Uh, what was it again, Itsuki?"

Everyone's attention suddenly turned to Koizumi, who responded without any sign of losing his composure.

"A frank person, I believe. That's what I remember telling you."

"We'll go with that then. Yes, I'd heard that you were more of a frank girl."

"Oh, really?"

Haruhi promptly dropped the invisible good girl mask. Then she flashed that brilliant smile she rarely showed outside the club room.

"Nice to meet ya, big guy! Moving right along, have any strange incidents happened in this mansion? And do the locals have a special name for the island or any ominous legends about the place? I happen to be interested in that kind of stuff."

Don't reveal your eccentric tastes to somebody you're meeting for the first time. And yeah, you shouldn't be telling the owner of the house that you want something bad to happen. What if he turns us away?

However, Keiichi Tamaru merely laughed generously.

"I happen to share your interests, but nothing has happened yet, since the building was only completed a few days ago. And I don't know anything about the history of the island. Though

I haven't heard anything particularly sinister about the place. After all, it was a deserted island."

And after that magnanimous gesture of kindness, he motioned for us to go inside.

"Let's not stand here and talk. Please come inside. This is a Western-style house so feel free to leave your shoes on. I suppose we should start by showing you to your rooms. Normally, I would ask Arakawa to serve as your guide, but he appears to be busy carrying stuff in. Guess I'll have to do it myself."

And with that, Keiichi led us inside.

Well, I'd like to provide a diagram of the interior of the villa that showed room assignments, but I learned that I had no talent for drawing back during the early years of grade school, so I'll refrain. Simply put, the rooms were staying in were on the second floor while Keiichi's bedroom and Yutaka's guest room were on the third floor. Perhaps that tells you how close they were. Arakawa the butler and Mori the maid were staying in smaller rooms on the first floor...

And that should cover everyone.

"Does this house have a name of some sort?"

Keiichi smiled wryly in response to Haruhi's question.

"It was just completed so we haven't thought of one yet. We're open to any good ideas."

"Yes. How does House of Tragedy or House of Fear sound? And you can name each room with names like Bloodsucking Hall or Cursed Room."

"Oh, that sounds great. I'll have nameplates made up for next time."

I really don't want to sleep in a room with a name that'll give me nightmares.

Our group passed through the lobby and up the stairs made of high-grade wood to reach the second floor. The hallway was lined with doors as though this were a hotel.

"The rooms should all be the same size, though. There are single and double rooms. Feel free to use whichever one you want."

Well, what to do? I wouldn't mind sharing a room, though with five of us, somebody's going to be left over, and logic dictates that Nagato would be the odd one out. Of course, I could offer to be Nagato's roommate and she probably wouldn't mind, but I'd end up instantly dying from an offhand punch by Haruhi.

"Well, we can each stay in our own room."

That was Koizumi's final conclusion.

"Since we'll only be in our rooms when we're sleeping anyway. And we're free to move between rooms. By the way, do the doors lock?"

"Of course."

Keiichi Tamaru smiled as he nodded.

"The keys are on the sideboard in each room. The doors don't lock automatically so you won't be locked out of your room if you forget the key, but I'd appreciate it if you didn't lose it."

I won't even need a key. I'll leave the door unlocked when I'm sleeping. Since Asahina might sneak in for some reason after everybody else has fallen asleep. And I don't have anything worth stealing with me. Nobody's going to commit theft in a situation with such a short suspect list. And if somebody did, it would obviously be Haruhi.

"Then I'll go check on Arakawa and Mori. Feel free to use this opportunity to explore the premises. Don't forget to check where the emergency exits are located. I'll be going then."

And with that, Keiichi returned downstairs.

Here was Haruhi's impression of Keiichi Tamaru.

"The absence of anything suspicious about him makes him a suspicious character."

"Then what if he looked suspicious?"

"There you go. He'd obviously be a suspicious character."

So as far as she's concerned, nothing in this world can be considered free of suspicion. Standards so strict the International Organization for Standardization would be surprised. She should work for the Japan Advertising Review Organization, Inc., in the future. She'd be busy with work every day.

We randomly chose rooms and unloaded our belongings before meeting up in the double room Haruhi had taken. Occupying a double room by herself definitely fell into the category of Haruhi-like behavior. In other words, her personality doesn't allow for any restraint or modesty.

The three girls were sitting on the bed, I was parked on the dressing table, and Koizumi was calmly leaning against the wall with his arms crossed.

"I've figured it out!"

Haruhi shouted all of a sudden and I reflexively responded in the usual fashion.

"Figured what out?"

"The culprit."

Haruhi's face as she made her proclamation seemed to be filled with some kind of mysterious conviction.

I reluctantly voiced what the other three were thinking.

"What culprit? Nothing's happened yet. We just got here."

"My gut tells me that the culprit is the master of this place. His first victim will probably be Mikuru."

"Eek!"

Asahina was really scared. She trembled like a little rabbit hearing the flapping of a hawk's wings and clutched at the skirt of Nagato, standing next to her. Nagato didn't say anything.

"..."

She just silently stared at a fixed point in the air.

"Like I said, what culprit?" I asked one more time. "Or should I say, what crime do you intend to blame Keiichi Tamaru for?"

"How am I supposed to know that? He just had a look in his eyes like he was plotting something. My gut is usually right. I'm sure that we'll be involved in some kind of big surprise."

I hoped that she was just talking about a simple surprise party, but Haruhi wasn't expecting a cheap birthday party with a lame catch.

Just imagine. Keiichi suddenly dropping the friendly smile and getting a crazy look in his eyes as he starts slashing guests with a kitchen knife. The old guy beating at the door to use us as sacrifices because he was possessed by an ancient spirit after stumbling upon an old dolmen deep in the forest of the island.

"That's ridiculous."

I waved one hand in a horizontal motion as I shot myself down.

There's no way that an acquaintance of Koizumi's would do something like that. The "Agency" can't be made up of a bunch of idiots. They should have investigated the site beforehand. Koizumi still has that usual harmless smile on his face. Arakawa the butler, Sonoh Mori, and Yutaka Tamaru have absolutely nothing in common with the residents from horror stories. Besides, Haruhi is looking for a detective mystery, not a splatter film.

If anything were to happen, it'd be a serial murder or two, right? Though I doubt it's going to happen so conveniently. The skies are clear and they haven't issued a high seas warning. This island hasn't become an isolated space.

Besides, Haruhi wouldn't truly wish for someone to die. If

Haruhi were that kind of a person, I'd have run out of patience after dealing with her for so long.

Haruhi, paying no heed to my worries, spoke up in an innocent-sounding voice. "Let's start by taking a swim. It wouldn't be a stretch to say that people come to the beach for the sole purpose of swimming. Let's see how far we can swim. We can have a contest to see who gets carried away by the waves first!"

Sure, but you better have a search and rescue team standing by.

Still, we just got here and we're already on the move? Hasn't she even considered taking a short break after the long voyage? Of course, it was possible that Haruhi wasn't tired, but she could at least occasionally refrain from using herself as the standard for everyone else.

"What are you talking about? You could take an offering to the Temple of Apollo, but that isn't going to stop the sun. We have to move before the sun sets 'cause time's a-wasting."

Haruhi wrapped her arms around Asahina and Nagato's necks.

"Wah," went Asahina as she blinked, while "..." was the silent response from Nagato.

"Swimsuits. Swimsuits. Get changed and meet up in the lobby. Heh-heh-heh. I chose the swimsuits these girls will be wearing. Kyon, you're getting excited, aren't you?"

Haruhi bared her white teeth with a creepy smirk in a look that said she knew what I was thinking.

"You're absolutely right."

I puffed my chest up in defiance. That was my primary objective for this trip. I won't let anyone rain on my parade.

"Koizumi, the private beach is reserved for us, right?!"

"Yes, that's right. Our only company will be a few seashells washed up on the shore. It's an unexplored beach. But the tide comes in quickly so you shouldn't get too far away from the coast. Assuming you were serious about having a contest."

"As if. It was just a joke. Someone like Mikuru would end up as fish food after getting swept away by the Kuroshio Current in no time. Okay, everybody? Don't get all excited and swim too far out. Stay where I can see you."

Should Haruhi be acting as the guardian here when she's the most excited one? Maybe I should suck it up and play that role. In any case, I'll take care not to let Asahina out of my sight for longer than two seconds.

"Over there! Kyon!"

Haruhi pointed her finger at the tip of my nose.

"Get that creepy smile off your face. You look better with your mouth half-open in a grimace. I won't be letting you have the camera!"

The high-flying and audacious Haruhi Express smiled.

"Okay, let's go!"

And so, here we are.

Here was a coastal beach of sand. The intense sunlight was definitely what you'd expect of summer. The advancing waves washed over the sand as white clouds puffy like cotton candy slowly floated across a canvas of deep blue. A sharp sea breeze rustled our hair and slowly beckoned us to the water.

The words "private beach" have a nice ring, but the truth was that there wasn't any need to book a reservation for this beach because it was on an island so far removed from civilization that nobody would ever bother coming here to swim, with the exception of foreign tourists who'd been fooled by some travel magazine. Needless to say, there wasn't any sign of human life around besides the five of us. There weren't even any birds flying around.

Which meant that the only witnesses lucky enough to see

Haruhi and the other girls in their swimsuits were the barnacles attached to the rocks. If you don't count Koizumi and me.

I had spread a blanket under the beach umbrella and squinted at Asahina, who looked all embarrassed, when Haruhi ran up to block my view.

"Mikuru, swimming at the beach is a rule of this world. Come on, let's go. It's unhealthy to stay out of the sunlight!"

"Wait, but my skin gets sunburned really easily…"

Haruhi paid no heed to Asahina's cowering as she led the pale upperclassman to the edge of the water and dove in.

"Wah, it's salty."

Asahina was surprised by the obvious as she splashed in the water.

As for Nagato.

"…"

She was kneeling on the blanket with her back straight, also in a swimsuit, as she read a paperback in silence.

"Each person has a different method of having fun."

Koizumi stopped blowing up the beach ball to smile at me.

"People should spend their leisure time doing activities they enjoy. Or else, that would defeat the point of going on a vacation. Shouldn't we attempt to relax and savor this four-day three-night trip?"

Isn't Haruhi the only one enjoying herself? I doubt that Asahina's feeling too relaxed when Haruhi's toying with her.

"Hey, Kyon! Koizumi! You guys get over here too!"

We stood up in response to Haruhi's sirenlike shouting. Truth be told, I didn't go reluctantly. Haruhi aside, my heart's desire was to be near Asahina. Koizumi passed the blown-up beach ball to me and I began walking across the hot sand.

Upon returning to the villa feeling moderately fatigued, we took quick showers before returning to our rooms for a brief rest, after which time the sky was filled with stars and Mori was leading us to the dining hall.

It was dinnertime.

Dinner that night was an extravagant affair. I doubt Asahina had particularly wanted to eat seafood, but there was a plateful in front of each of us, enough to make a person destined to live in poverty like me sit up straight. And we're getting free room and board? Is this really okay?

"Absolutely."

Keiichi Tamaru assured us with a smile on his face. "Just think of it as a way of showing my appreciation for coming all the way out here. After all, I was bored. Well, I don't mean that I would have invited anybody available. But Itsuki's friends are more than welcome here."

Keiichi was now dressed formally, unlike when he came out to greet us. He wore a dark suit with a necktie in a Windsor knot. The food being served was a mix of Japanese and European cuisine with a menu including carpaccio, meuniere, and some kind of steamed dish among others, though Keiichi was the only one eating with a knife and fork. The rest of us had been using chopsticks the whole time.

"The food is absolutely delicious. Who made this?" Haruhi asked as she displayed an appetite worthy of consideration for an eating contest.

"The butler, Arakawa, also serves as the chef. Impressive, isn't it?" said Keiichi.

"I'd love to offer my appreciation. Please call him over later."

Haruhi was putting on the airs of a person at a fancy restaurant.

Asahina's eyes widened every time she took a bite. Nagato, who

didn't seem like a big eater, was keeping up a surprising pace. Koizumi was cheerfully chatting with Yutaka and the others.

"Would you like something to drink?"

Mori, who served as our waitress in her maid outfit, held a long and narrow bottle as she smiled at me. Looks like some kind of wine. Can't say that I approve of offering alcohol to minors, but I decided to try a glass. I'd never had wine before, but humans are supposed to be a little adventurous. Besides, I'd feel bad if I turned down Mori while being faced with that charming smile.

"Ah, what are you drinking by yourself over there, Kyon? I want some of that too."

Per Haruhi's request, a glass of wine was passed to everyone.

Somehow, I have a feeling that this was when the nightmare began.

That day, I discovered that Asahina had absolutely zero tolerance for alcohol, Nagato was like a bottomless pit, and Haruhi was a hopeless drunk.

My own memories were rather hazy since I got cocky and drank a bit too much, but I recall Haruhi drinking from the bottle as she slapped Keiichi's head.

"Man, you're the best! I'll leave Mikuru here as thanks for inviting us. Do some serious maid training. This girl really needs help."

I vaguely remembered Haruhi shouting something along those lines.

The real maid, Sonoh Mori, had lined up the wine bottles on the table like bowling pins and presented us with expertly sliced apples for dessert. Asahina, the fake maid who was only on duty in the club room, was collapsed on the table, her face completely red.

Nagato continued emptying the alcoholic beverages Mori brought over. I had no idea how her body processed alcohol, but her complexion hadn't changed a bit as she emptied bottle after bottle like a whale drinking seawater.

Yutaka looked at her with great interest.

"Are you sure you're fine?"

The sight of him talking to Nagato in a concerned voice tugged at a corner of my memory.

That night, I completely passed out and was able to reach my bed only with Koizumi's help. Koizumi told me afterward with a mocking smile on his face. He also mentioned that I, along with Haruhi, had engaged in some sort of disgraceful behavior, but I had no recollection of any such thing, so I'll just pretend that I never heard him tell me that. We'll just say it was one of Koizumi's typical jokes.

Because what happened the next day pushed all that stuff to the corners of our minds.

On the morning of the second day, a storm showed up out of the blue.

A horizontal rain pounded on the walls as strong gusts howled ominously. The trees around the villa shook as though they were possessed by ghosts.

"Rotten luck. A hurricane had to show up now of all times," Haruhi muttered as she looked out the window. We were in Haruhi's room. We had gathered to hold a meeting to discuss what we would do today.

We had already eaten breakfast. Keiichi had been absent from the table that morning. Apparently, he had a hard time getting up in the morning, and it was all but impossible for him to get out of bed before noon, according to Arakawa's explanation.

Haruhi turned to us.

"But you know. Now we're really on a remote island in the middle of a storm. A once-in-a-lifetime situation. Maybe something will actually happen."

Asahina flinched as her eyes darted around. Koizumi and Nagato looked as though this was business as usual.

The waves had been perfectly calm yesterday, yet now we had a high wave warning. Definitely beyond acceptable conditions for going out in a boat. If it's still this bad in two days, we'll have been unwillingly trapped on this island because of Haruhi's will. A closed circle. It couldn't be.

Koizumi smiled in an attempt to reassure us.

"It appears to be a fast-moving hurricane so conditions should improve over the next two days. It'll suddenly disappear the way it suddenly showed up."

"That's what the weather forecast says. But there wasn't any information about a hurricane coming yesterday. Whose head did this storm happen to pop out of?"

"It was a coincidence," Koizumi said calmly. "An ordinary natural phenomenon. One of the signs of summer. We get at least one large-scale hurricane every year."

"I was planning on exploring the island, but we'll have to cancel that," Haruhi said in a bitter voice. "Can't do anything about that. Let's find something we can do indoors."

I guess that Haruhi had completely forgotten the purpose of this trip since her focus had shifted to having fun. I appreciated the change, since I didn't want to cross over to the other side of the island to find the carcass of some huge organism washed up against the cliff.

Koizumi offered his opinion.

"I believe there is a game room. I'll ask Keiichi to let us use it.

Would you prefer mahjong or billiards? I'm sure they could also prepare a Ping-Pong table if we asked."

Haruhi approved.

"Then we'll have a Ping-Pong tournament. A round-robin tournament to determine the first SOS Brigade Ping-Pong champion. The loser has to buy juice for everyone on the ferry ride back. You're not allowed to hold yourself back."

The game room was in the basement. It was a spacious hall with mahjong and billiard tables in addition to a roulette wheel and baccarat table. Were Koizumi's relatives running a casino on the side? This seemed to be a prime spot for gambling.

"Who knows?" Koizumi said with an innocent smile on his face. He was sliding a folded-up Ping-Pong table over from the wall.

Incidentally, Haruhi won the Ping-Pong tournament after a fiercely contested match with me. We then moved onto a mahjong tournament. However, Koizumi was the only SOS Brigade member who knew the rules, so it turned into a game of learn as we go. The Tamaru brothers joined in halfway through, which made the mahjong session a lot more animated. Haruhi distorted the rules to make up her own winning hands that didn't make any sense, like "Two Color One Void" and "Pseudo-Outside Hand" and "Permanently Two Away," and declare victory after victory. It was amusing so we let her have her fun. Plus we weren't playing for money.

"*Ron!* Probably around ten thousand points!"

"Suzumiya, that's capped at eight thousand."

I surreptitiously released a sigh of relief. I should have adopted a more optimistic mind-set. It would be best to enjoy this trip in a normal fashion. At this rate, there wouldn't be any fishy sea monsters popping out of the ocean or any aboriginals storming out of the forest. After all, we were on a remote island in the middle of the ocean. Nothing weird would be able to come from the outside.

With that in mind, I decided to relax. Keiichi Tamaru and Yutaka along with the Arakawa-Mori servant combo appeared quite normal for acquaintances of Koizumi. We would need a few more characters before anything strange could happen.

That's what I wanted to believe.

But as they say, it ain't over till the fat lady sings. I don't know exactly which fat lady is doing the singing or where she's planning on doing her singing, but once I find out where she is, I'd love to put her out of commission for a whole year.

The trouble came on the morning of the third day.

We spent the second day having fun and gorging ourselves, and the weather got even worse that night as we held a banquet so similar to the previous night it was like a replay. On the third day, I woke up with a killer headache. If Koizumi hadn't woken us up, Haruhi, Asahina, and I would probably have kept on sleeping.

I opened the curtains. The storm was still pouring down on us on the morning of the third day.

"I wonder if we'll be able to go home tomorrow."

I splashed cold water on my face to clear my head until I could walk in a straight line and carefully walked downstairs, making sure I didn't trip.

The other members were already sitting at the table in the dining hall. Haruhi and Asahina looked about as bad as I did while Nagato and Koizumi looked the same as always.

The brothers Keiichi Tamaru and Yutaka weren't here yet. They might have reached their limit after consecutive hangovers. I recalled Haruhi turning the bottle upside down over their glasses. Haruhi was arrogant enough under normal circumstances, but alcohol only served to power her up to unrivaled levels of recklessness, which only made my head hurt more. I resolved to never drink alcohol again with such reckless abandon.

"I'm going to stop drinking wine."

It appeared that Haruhi had learned her lesson yesterday as she made her declaration with a grimace on her face.

"For some reason, I have no memory of what happened after dinner. Isn't that an incredible waste? It's like I lost that time. Yeah, I'm never going to get drunk again. We're going alcohol-free tonight."

Normally, high school students shouldn't be drinking anyway, so I suppose I should praise Haruhi for a relatively decent proposal. But yeah, Asahina in a drunken daze was pretty damn sexy so I couldn't say that we should get rid of alcohol altogether.

"Let's do that then."

Koizumi immediately agreed with her like a sycophant as Mori came in with the cart that had our breakfast.

"Could you refrain from serving alcohol tonight? Soft drinks only, please."

"Understood."

Mori bowed respectfully as she set plates of bacon and eggs on the table.

The Tamaru brothers had yet to show up in the dining hall by the time we'd finished eating. We knew that Keiichi had an extremely hard time getting up in the morning, but Yutaka's absence was somewhat odd.

"Everyone."

Arakawa and Mori appeared before us. I could sense that

Arakawa's composed face was slightly disturbed. I had a really bad feeling.

"What is it?" Koizumi asked him. "Is there something wrong?"

"Yes," said Arakawa. "Something that could be considered a problem may have happened. A short while ago, Mori went to check Master Yutaka's room."

Mori slowly nodded before she picked up where the butler had left off.

"The room wasn't locked so I went inside, but Master Yutaka was nowhere to be found."

She spoke in a voice that sounded like bells ringing. Mori stared at the tablecloth as she spoke.

"The room was completely empty. There were no signs that the bed had been slept in."

"And then I tried to reach the master over the intercom. However, there was no response."

Arakawa's words made Haruhi drop the glass of orange juice in her hand.

"What's that? So Yutaka is missing and Keiichi isn't responding?"

"To be frank, that would be correct," said Arakawa.

"You can't get into Keiichi's room? Isn't there an extra key?"

"I hold the spare keys for the other rooms, but the master's room is an exception. The master holds the only spare key. It's a precaution since there are documents concerning his work inside."

The bad feeling gnawing at my gut had expanded into a dark cloud covering a third of my spirit. The master of the manor who wouldn't wake up. The younger brother who had disappeared.

Arakawa bowed ever so slightly.

"I intend to proceed to the master's room now. If possible, I'd like everyone to accompany me. I sense a sort of unrest. Though I hope my worries are for naught."

Haruhi shot me a quick look. Is she trying to tell me something?
"We should go take a look."
Koizumi immediately stood up.
"He could be ill or in some other condition which is preventing him from getting up. It may be necessary to break the door down."
Haruhi hopped out of her seat.
"Kyon, let's go. I've got a bad feeling about this. Come on, Yuki and Mikuru too!"
The look on Haruhi's face was extraordinarily serious.

I'll make this quick.
We knocked on the door to Keiichi's bedroom on the third floor but there wasn't any response. Koizumi turned the knob but the solid oak door wouldn't open and stood like a wall that impeded our progress.
We'd checked Yutaka Tamaru's room on the way there, but just as Mori said, the bedsheets were untouched, making it highly unlikely that anybody had spent the night in that room. Where had he gone? Were he and Keiichi both cooped up in Keiichi's room?
"If the door is locked from the inside, that means there must be someone in the room."
Koizumi stroked his chin as he put on a thinking face before speaking in an unusually terse voice.
"We have no choice. We must break down the door. Time could become a critical factor, depending on the situation."
And so we bunched together and repeatedly slammed into the door. We being Koizumi, Arakawa, and myself. Nagato could probably pick the lock or something, but we couldn't let her use her funky magic in front of all these people. The three female members of the SOS Brigade and Mori the maid watched from

the side as we three males slammed into the door again and again. My shoulder blade was on the verge of screaming in pain when—

The door finally sprang open.

The momentum carried Koizumi, Arakawa, and me into the room, where we fell down, and then—

Yes, we have now returned to the opening scene. Finally returned to the present. Back to telling the story in real time.

. . . .

. . . . . .

. . .

And once that flashback had concluded, I lifted myself off the floor. I looked away from Keiichi, who lay with a knife stuck in him, to scrutinize the door with the busted lock. I marveled at the sturdiness of the newly built mansion; even the doors were shiny...or yeah, I'm trying to escape reality here.

Arakawa kneeled next to his master's body and placed his fingertips against Keiichi's neck. He then looked up at us.

"He has passed on," he said in a composed voice, perhaps because he was a professional.

"Ah, ahhh..."

Asahina's legs had given out and she was sitting out in the hallway. I suppose that was only natural. I felt like doing the same. Nagato's expressionless face was feeling like a real blessing right about now.

"It appears that we're in quite a predicament."

Koizumi circled around Keiichi to the side opposite Arakawa. Koizumi crouched down, carefully reached out, and gingerly touched the jacket of Keiichi's suit.

His white shirt was stained by a dark red liquid blot of irregular shape.

"Oh?" Koizumi said in a dubious voice.

I looked over. There was a notepad in Keiichi's shirt pocket. The knife had gone through the suit and pierced the notepad before entering his body. The person who committed this act of violence must have been fairly strong. It doesn't appear that the ladies here would have been capable of such an act. Though I suppose Haruhi and her ridiculous strength could have pulled it off.

Koizumi spoke in a pensive voice.

"Our first priority is to preserve the scene of the crime. For now, let's leave the room."

"Mikuru, are you okay?"

It wasn't that surprising for Haruhi to sound concerned since Asahina had apparently fainted. She was sitting on the floor with her eyes closed and leaning against Nagato's thin legs.

"Yuki, we'll carry Mikuru to my room. You take that arm."

I suppose that Haruhi talking like a person with common sense could be considered a sign of how upset she was. Nagato and Haruhi each grabbed one of Asahina's arms and dragged her off toward the stairs.

Once I was sure they were gone, I turned to survey my surroundings.

Arakawa's hands were clasped in prayer over his master and he had a grieved expression on his face. Mori stood to the side, looking down in sorrow. And Yutaka Tamaru was still nowhere to be found. It was storming outside.

"Well, then," Koizumi said to me with a thin smile back on his face. "Have you noticed? This situation is exactly what you would call a closed circle."

I already knew that.

"And at first glance, it would appear that we have a murder on our hands."

Since this doesn't look like a suicide.

"Furthermore, it happened in a sealed room."

I turned to look at the locked windows.

"How could the culprit commit the crime in this inaccessible room and make his escape?"

Ask the culprit.

"Indeed," Koizumi concurred. "We'll need to ask Yutaka about this matter."

Koizumi instructed Arakawa to call the police, then he turned back to me.

"Please go on ahead to Suzumiya's room. I'll be there shortly."

That seemed like a good idea. There wasn't anything I could do here.

I knocked on the door.

"Who is it?"

"It's me."

The door opened a crack and Haruhi peeked out. She invited me in with a strained look on her face.

"Where's Koizumi?"

"He should be here soon."

Asahina was sleeping on one of the two beds. You didn't have to be a prince passing by to want to kiss that sleeping face, but she had a pained expression and she was still unconscious, so I couldn't do anything about it.

Nagato was sitting in a chair next to her like someone keeping watch over a tomb. Keep it up. Don't leave Asahina's side.

"Say, what do you think?"

Haruhi's question appeared to be directed at me.

"What do you mean?"

"Keiichi. Is this a murder case?"

If one views one's current situation from an objective stand-point, one should be able to derive the answer. I gave it a try. We broke down the locked door to find the master of the manor lying completely still on the floor with the handle of a knife sticking out of his chest. A murder in a sealed room on a remote island in the middle of a storm. Too perfect.

"Looks like it."

After a few seconds of time lag, Haruhi sighed in response to my answer.

"Hmm..."

Haruhi lifted one hand to her forehead as she plopped down on her bed.

"Unbelievable. I never expected something like this to happen."

Her murmured words were also hard to believe. Weren't you talking about how badly you wanted something to happen?

"That's 'cause I wasn't expecting something to actually happen."

Haruhi grimaced before quickly changing her expression. She appeared to be worrying about what to do in her own way. I was relieved that she wasn't celebrating. Since I wouldn't want to end up playing the role of the second victim.

I looked at the upperclassman sleeping with the face of an angel.

"How's Asahina doing?"

"She should be fine. She just fainted. I have to admire her meek reaction. It's just like Mikuru to faint. Though at least she didn't go into hysterics."

Haruhi's mind appeared to be elsewhere as she spoke.

A murder in a sealed room on a remote island during a storm.

What were the chances of such a thing happening during our trip? However, we were the SOS Brigade, not an occult society or a mystery novel association. Though according to Haruhi, the core principle of the SOS Brigade was to search for the supernatural. Our present circumstances somewhat matched that principle, though I have to say that it's a totally different story once you're actually experiencing something happening.

Did this happen because Haruhi desired so?

"Hmm. This isn't good…"

Haruhi got up from the bed and began pacing around the room.

She reminded me of a mischievous boy after an April Fool's prank gone wrong. Like a person joking around about something bad happening and then it actually happened. I didn't feel too good myself.

Well, what to do?

I would have loved to go to sleep next to Asahina, but it wouldn't be very productive to escape reality. We needed to come up with a way to deal with this. I wonder what Koizumi planned on doing.

"Yeah, I can't just sit around waiting," Haruhi said in a firm voice as she stood before me.

I suppose I should have expected this. Haruhi had a serious expression on her face as she shot me a challenging look.

"I need to check something. Kyon, you come with me."

"I don't want to leave Asahina here like this."

"Yuki's with her so she'll be fine. Yuki, you lock the door and don't open it for anyone. Got it?"

Nagato coolly stared at Haruhi.

"Yes."

She responded in a monotone voice.

Her lifeless eyes met mine for a brief instant. She nodded ever so slightly at an angle where only I would notice—I think.

I doubted that anything dangerous would happen to Haruhi and me. If something were to happen to worsen this situation, Nagato wouldn't be sitting there silently. As proof I recalled the memory of when we went to the computer society president's room a short while back.

"Let's go, Kyon."

Haruhi grabbed my wrist before stepping out of the room and into the hallway.

"So where are we going?"

"Keiichi's room. I didn't have time to look around earlier so I want to check the scene again."

I recalled Keiichi lying on the floor with a knife in his chest and the dried blood sticking to his white shirt and hesitated for a moment. That's not something you want to stare too closely at.

Haruhi continued to talk as she walked.

"And we need to find out where Yutaka went. He may still be in the building. Besides…"

We caused quite a commotion. If Yutaka had nothing to do with the murder, it would be quite odd for him not to show himself. There could be only two possible reasons for his absence.

I spoke up as Haruhi dragged me up the stairs.

"Either Yutaka was the culprit and already escaped the villa or Yutaka was also a victim…right?"

"Yep. But things could get ugly if Yutaka isn't the culprit."

"I'd say that they're already ugly enough regardless of who the culprit is…"

Haruhi gave me a sideways glance.

"Hey, Kyon. Excluding the Tamaru brothers, the only people in this manor would be Arakawa, Mori, and the five of us. That would mean the culprit is one of those people. I don't want to suspect my own brigade members or turn them over to the police."

She sounded awfully solemn.

I see. She's worried that one of us was the killer. I hadn't even considered that possibility. Asahina was out of the question and Nagato would have done a better job. As for Koizumi... Now that I think about it, Koizumi had been the closest one to Tamaru. He'd mentioned being a relative. That would make him much more relevant than complete strangers like the rest of us.

"No."

I poked myself in the head.

Koizumi wasn't an idiot. He wouldn't purposely commit such borderline acts in this kind of situation. I doubt that he would be crazy enough to commit a murder just because we happened to be in a closed circle.

Haruhi's the only crazy person we need around here.

Arakawa the butler was standing erect in front of Keiichi's room on the third floor.

"I contacted the police and was instructed not to allow anyone inside."

He bowed respectfully. The doorway was still open since we'd broken down the door, and we could see Keiichi's toes through the space under Arakawa's arms.

"When will the police get here?"

Arakawa responded politely to Haruhi's question. "It depends on when the storm passes. According to the forecast, the weather will have improved by tomorrow afternoon, so I suppose they will arrive sometime in that vicinity."

"Hmm."

Haruhi kept glancing into the room. "I have a few questions."

"What would you like to know?"

"Did Keiichi and Yutaka not get along?"

Arakawa shifted slightly from his perfect butler posture.

"To be honest, I do not know. For I have only been working here for the past week."

"The past week?" Haruhi and I asked.

Arakawa slowly nodded. "That would be correct. I am, in fact, an actual butler, though I was merely hired to be a part-time, temporary butler. Our contract was for a brief two weeks during this summer."

"So it was just for this villa? You weren't previously employed by Keiichi?"

"That would be correct."

Arakawa the butler was only serving as Keiichi's butler while they were on this island. That opens up some possibilities.

It appeared that Haruhi had the same question I did.

"Does the same go for Mori? Was she also a temporarily hired maid?"

"It is just as you say. She was hired at the same time."

That's rather bold. Keiichi hired a butler and maid solely for this summer vacation. I have a feeling that wasn't the best way to spend his money. Still, a butler and maid, huh...

A minuscule doubt was tugging at the edge of my mind and on the verge of falling off. I scooped it back up. And then I took a careful look at Arakawa's face. All I could see was an old gentleman who was the definition of sincere. That was probably the correct judgment call, but still...?

I kept my mouth shut and smothered that doubt. I'll have to toss this question to that guy when I see him later.

"I see. So there can be permanent and temporary servants. That information should be very helpful."

Helpful for what? Haruhi nodded as though she'd just figured something out.

"There's nothing for us to do here if we can't go in the room. Kyon, let's move on."

She took my arm again and stomped off.

"Where are we going this time?"

"Outside. To check if the boat's there."

I can't say I'm very inclined to walk through the middle of a hurricane with Haruhi.

"You see, I only believe what I see with my own eyes. Information that's passed around through hearsay tends to be distorted. Understood? Kyon. It's critical to obtain information from a primary source. Information from secondary sources that have gone through other hands cannot be trusted."

Yeah, I suppose that's a reasonable view, but you'll end up unable to trust anything outside your own little world.

While I considered the usefulness of information media, Haruhi dragged me to the first floor, where we ran into Sonoh Mori.

"Are you going outside?" Mori asked Haruhi and me.

Haruhi responded, "Yep. We're going to check if the boat is there."

"I don't believe it is."

"Why?"

Mori smiled thinly before answering.

"It was last night. Master Yutaka appeared to be in a hurry as he headed for the entrance."

Haruhi and I exchanged glances.

"So you're saying that Yutaka took the boat and left the island?"

Mori continued smiling thinly as her lips moved.

"I only happened to pass him in the hallway and never actually saw Master Yutaka go outside. However, that was the last time I saw Master Yutaka."

"What time was it?" asked Haruhi.

"I believe it was around one AM."

We would have been inebriated and sound asleep at the time.

Was this confirmation that the suit-clad Keiichi had collapsed on the floor around the same time?

We opened the door, to be pelted by raindrops. Once we managed to squeeze past the door, which barely budged because of the gale force winds, Haruhi and I were completely soaked within a matter of seconds. Guess I should have just worn my swimsuit.

The gray cloudy sky looming over our heads with no end in sight reminded me of being in closed space. I guess I'm just not very fond of the concept of a monochrome world.

"Let's go."

Haruhi gallantly advanced through the rain with her hair and T-shirt sticking to her body because of it. I had no choice but to follow. Haruhi's hand was still gripped around my wrist.

We would probably be launched into the air by this wind if we had wings. Helpless against the pouring rain, we made our way until we could see the wharf. There was the possibility of falling off the cliff if we weren't careful. Even I was starting to feel the danger in this situation. I didn't want to fall by myself so I grabbed Haruhi's wrist in return. I figured that I'd have a higher chance of surviving a fall if I was with her.

We finally reached the top of the stairs.

"Can you see, Kyon?"

Haruhi's words were almost carried away by the wind. I nodded in response.

"Yeah."

The wharf was practically submerged as giant wave after giant wave crashed against the bank.

"The boat's gone. If it wasn't washed away, somebody took it and left."

Our only means of getting off this island. I looked across the sea but the fancy cruiser was nowhere to be seen.

Golly gee.

And so, we were now stranded on this remote island.

We returned to the villa at the same snail's pace. By the time we made it inside the door, we were both completely wet.

"Please use these."

Mori had apparently been waiting thoughtfully as she handed us towels before continuing in a reserved voice.

"Did you find anything?"

"It was just like you said."

Haruhi had a disappointed look on her face as she dried her black hair.

"The cruiser was gone. We don't know when it disappeared, though."

Mori continued to smile like the glow of a firefly. Not sure if that was just how she naturally looked. If she was upset by the death of Keiichi Tamaru, it was hidden underneath her calm and professional demeanor. Though I suppose this would be the normal reaction from a temporarily hired maid.

As we apologized to Mori for dripping water all over the hallway, Haruhi and I returned to our respective rooms for a change of clothes.

"Come to my room when you're finished," Haruhi said on our way up the stairs.

"It's better to stay together in these situations. I'll worry if I don't have my eyes on everyone. Besides, on the off chance that…"

Haruhi shut her mouth as she was about to say something. Somehow, I had a feeling that I knew what she was going to say, so I didn't say anything.

We reached the second floor to find Koizumi standing in the hallway.

"We appreciate you going out in this weather."

Koizumi had his usual smile on his face as he nodded in our direction. We were in front of Haruhi's room.

"What are you doing?"

Koizumi's smile grew strained as he shrugged in response to Haruhi's question.

"I came to Suzumiya's room to discuss what we would do next, but Nagato wouldn't let me in."

"Why not?"

"I don't have the slightest idea."

Haruhi pounded on the door.

"Yuki, it's me. Open the door."

After a brief moment of silence, we heard Nagato's voice through the door.

"I was told not to open the door for anyone."

It would seem that Asahina was still unconscious. Haruhi fiddled with the towel draped around her neck.

"It's okay now. Yuki, open up."

"That would require me to violate the order to not open the door for anyone."

Haruhi looked at me with her jaw dropped before turning back to the door.

"Okay, Yuki. When I said anyone, I meant anyone besides us. Kyon, Koizumi, and I don't count. We're all in the SOS Brigade together, right?"

"That was never mentioned. I have interpreted the order to mean that I should not open the door for anybody at all."

Nagato's soft voice sounded like a priestess reading an oracle to a scribe.

"Hey, Nagato."

I couldn't put up with this any longer so I cut in.

"Haruhi's order has been rescinded. Or here, I'll override her order. Just open the door. Please."

Nagato spent a few seconds thinking on the other side of the wooden door. Then there was a click as the door unlocked and slowly opened.

"..."

Nagato's eyes passed over the area above us before she silently retreated into the room.

"Geez! Yuki, you need to be more flexible. You should be able to understand what I mean."

Haruhi told Koizumi to wait for her to get changed before entering the room. I was also dying for some dry clothes. I'll back off for now.

"See ya, Koizumi."

As I walked away, I had a sudden thought.

Was that whole exchange supposed to be Nagato's idea of a joke? If that were the case, it was a pretty lame attempt at wordplay and not very funny.

Give me a break, Nagato. Your face and expression never change so I can only assume that you're always serious. You could at least smile when you're telling a joke. You could even smile for no reason the way Koizumi does. I guarantee you'll look better that way.

Except that now isn't the time to be smiling.

I took off my wet clothes and also changed my underwear before going back out into the hallway to find that Koizumi was no longer outside. I went to Haruhi's room and knocked on the door.

"It's me."

The door was opened by Koizumi. I stepped inside and shut the door behind me.

"So it seems that the cruiser was gone."

Koizumi was leaning against the wall.

Haruhi sat cross-legged on the bed. Even Haruhi couldn't find any joy in the current situation as she looked up sullenly with a listless expression on her face.

"It wasn't there, right, Kyon?"

"Yeah," I said.

Koizumi spoke next.

"It appears that somebody took it and escaped. No, there's no point in being ambiguous. The one who escaped was Yutaka."

"How do you know?" I asked.

"Nobody else could have done it," Koizumi answered coolly.

"Nobody else was invited to this island and the only guest missing from the manor is Yutaka. It doesn't matter how you look at it. He must have stolen the boat and made a run for it."

Koizumi continued in a smooth voice.

"In other words, Yutaka was the culprit. He probably escaped while it was still dark."

Based on the fact that there had been no signs of anyone sleeping in Yutaka's bed and Mori's testimony.

Haruhi informed Koizumi of the previous conversation.

"As impressive as always, Suzumiya. You've already heard from her."

Koizumi engaged in his ass-kissing while I snorted for no real reason.

"Yutaka appeared to be in a hurry as though he was frightened of something. That would match the testimony from the last witness to see him. I also checked with Arakawa."

Even so, heading out to sea in the middle of the night during a hurricane would practically be suicide, wouldn't it?

"Something may have happened which created the need to escape in a hurry. Such as the need to flee the scene of a murder."

"Does Yutaka know how to operate a cruiser?"

"I was unable to verify that information, but we can draw our own conclusion from the end result. Since the boat is gone."

"Hold it right there!"

Haruhi raised her hand for the right to speak.

"What about the door to Keiichi's room? Who locked it? Was that also Yutaka's work?"

"Not necessarily," Koizumi gently refuted her. "As Arakawa said, Keiichi possessed both the key to the room and the spare. Further investigation revealed that both keys were within the room."

"Someone could have made a duplicate."

I tossed that idea into the fray. Koizumi shook his head.

"This was Yutaka's first visit to the manor. I doubt he would have had the time to make a duplicate."

Koizumi spread his arms in a sign of defeat.

A hush fell over the room as the clashing sounds of strong winds and pouring rain faded into the background.

Haruhi and I waited in silence, unable to find anything to say, until it was broken by Koizumi.

"However, there would be a slight discrepancy if Yutaka committed the crime last night."

"What do you mean?" asked Haruhi.

"When I touched Keiichi earlier, his skin was still warm. As though he had still been alive a short while ago."

Koizumi suddenly smiled. And then he turned to the reticent specter who stood next to Asahina like an attendant.

"Nagato, what was Keiichi's body temperature when we found him?"

"Ninety-seven point thirty-four degrees."

Nagato responded without missing a beat.

Hold on, Nagato. How do you know that without ever touching him? And you answered instantly, as though you had been expecting the question...but I didn't say any of that out loud.

The one person who might have questioned the prior exchange was Haruhi, but she must have been too busy thinking since she didn't notice anything wrong.

"That's practically normal body temperature. When was the crime committed then?"

"The body temperature of a human being after death drops around a couple degrees every hour. We can use this information to estimate that Keiichi died less than an hour before we found him."

"Wait, Koizumi."

I couldn't hold myself back this time.

"Didn't Yutaka run off while it was still night?"

"Yes, that's what I said."

"But the time of death was within an hour of finding the body?"

"That's how the numbers worked out."

I pressed my hand against my forehead.

"So Yutaka left the villa in the middle of the night during a hurricane and hid himself somewhere before returning in the morning to stab Keiichi and escape on the boat?"

"No, that would be incorrect."

He easily dodged that one.

"Even if we allow for a margin of error on the estimated time of death, we still have to assume that it happened around an hour before we found the body. However, we were already awake and in the dining hall by that time. But we didn't see any sign of Yutaka or even hear a single sound. Even with a hurricane outside, that would be unnatural."

"What does that mean?" Haruhi said in a sullen voice.

Her arms were crossed as she glared at Koizumi and me. You're not going to learn anything by glaring at me. If you want answers, tell the smiling boy next to me.

Koizumi continued in a light tone as though we were talking about the weather.

"This wasn't a sinister murder. It was merely a tragic accident."

"You don't look too upset about it."

"There is no doubt that Yutaka stabbed Keiichi. Or else there wouldn't be a reason for Yutaka to escape."

Well, that makes sense.

"I do not know the motive or circumstances involved, but Yutaka attacked Keiichi with a knife. He probably had it hidden behind his back as he came from the front. Keiichi had no time to brace himself so he was probably unable to resist at all when he was stabbed."

He sounds like he saw the whole thing happen.

"However, the tip of the knife had yet to reach his heart. I'm not sure it had even touched his skin. The knife was thrust into the notepad in Keiichi's chest pocket, meaning that the notepad was the only casualty."

"Huh? What do you mean?"

Haruhi's brow creased as she spoke.

"Then how did Keiichi die? Someone else killed him?"

"Nobody killed him. There was no killer in this case. Keiichi ended up that way purely by accident."

"What about Yutaka? Why did he run away?"

"Because he believed that he had killed Keiichi."

Koizumi answered calmly as he raised his index finger. Does he think he's one of those famous detectives?

"Allow me to explain my thinking. The sequence of events went as follows: Last night, Yutaka went to Keiichi's room with murderous intent and stabbed Keiichi with the knife. However, the knife was lodged in the notepad and didn't deliver a fatal wound."

I have no idea what he's getting at, but I'll just listen for now.

"However, this is when it got complicated. Keiichi believed that he had been stabbed. He still would have felt the force of the knife hitting the notepad. Furthermore, we can assume that he suffered a psychological shock at the sight of a knife sticking out of his own chest."

I was beginning to understand where Koizumi was going with this. Come on, now. No way.

"That misconception led to Keiichi fainting. When collapsing, he would have either fallen sideways or backwards."

Koizumi paused to take a breath.

"Upon witnessing Keiichi's collapse, Yutaka believed that he had killed him. What followed was simple. He could only escape. This wasn't a premeditated murder. Rather, he had merely used the knife in a heated moment of rage. So he stole the cruiser, despite it being nighttime in the middle of a storm."

"Huh? But then..."

Haruhi spoke up before Koizumi interrupted her.

"Please allow me to continue my explanation. The actions taken by the unconscious Keiichi afterwards. He remained unconscious until this morning. We were wondering why he hadn't woken up so we came to knock on the door to his room."

So he was still alive at that time...?

"The knocking on the door woke up Keiichi and he stumbled to the door. However, he must have been in a daze, considering how hard it was for him to get up in the morning. He was probably unable to think clearly. He was approaching the door half-asleep when he finally remembered."

"Remembered what?" Haruhi asked. Koizumi smiled at her.

"That his brother had tried to kill him. And once he recalled the sight of Yutaka with a knife in his hands, Keiichi promptly locked the door."

I couldn't hold myself back so I interjected.

"Don't tell me that's supposed to explain the whole sealed room deal."

"I'm afraid so. After being unconscious for so long, Keiichi had lost sense of time. He believed that Yutaka had returned. We were probably only a second or two late. The instant I grabbed the doorknob from the outside, it was locked from the inside."

"The killer wouldn't knock on the door if he came to finish him off."

"Keiichi's mind was still hazy so he made a poor spur-of-the-moment judgment since he wasn't thinking clearly."

That's some pretty arbitrary reasoning.

"And so, Keiichi backed away from the door after locking it. His instincts must have told him that he was in danger. That was when tragedy struck."

Koizumi shook his head the way a person would when telling a tragedy.

"Keiichi tripped over his feet and fell to the floor. Like this."

Koizumi bent his body as though he were falling forward.

"As a result, the knife stuck in the notepad near his chest was pushed into his body by the force of the handle hitting the floor and the blade pierced his heart, leaving him dead…"

Koizumi looked at Haruhi and me with our mouths wide open like idiots before he continued in a firm voice.

"That is what really happened."

What was that?

Keiichi died for such a stupid reason? How could everything happen so conveniently? The whole knife perfectly missing then not missing is one thing, but Yutaka should have realized if he'd killed Keiichi or not.

I prepared my rebuttal.

"Ah!" Haruhi suddenly shouted, which made me jump. Where'd that come from?

"Koizumi, but..." Haruhi said before freezing all of a sudden. Her face was filled with shock. Why was she shocked? Was there a part of Koizumi's story she couldn't accept?

Haruhi's eyes drifted over toward me. When her eyes met mine, she quickly looked away and turned back toward Koizumi before deciding against it and looking up at the ceiling for some odd reason.

"Eh...Never mind. I'm sure that's what happened. Mmm. How should I put it?"

After muttering incomprehensibly for a while, she fell silent.

Asahina was still asleep, while Nagato stared blankly at Koizumi.

For now, the meeting was adjourned. We returned to our individual rooms. According to Koizumi, the police would be coming once the storm calmed down so we should have our belongings packed up by that time.

After killing some time doing nothing in particular, I had come up with a number of questions so I headed to a certain room.

"What is the matter?"

Koizumi looked up from where he was folding his clothes and smiled at me.

"We need to talk."

There was one reason I had come to Koizumi's room.

"I can't accept it."

That's right. Koizumi's deduction hadn't explained everything. There were gaping holes.

"If we go by your explanation, the corpse should have been found facedown. But Keiichi was lying faceup. How do you explain that?"

Koizumi stood up from where he'd been sitting on his bed and turned to face me.

"There is a simple reason for that. The deduction I revealed to everyone was a false explanation."

I didn't show any visible reaction.

"Figures. The only one who would have eaten up that story was Asahina and she wasn't even conscious. I could just ask Nagato to tell me everything, but that'd feel like cheating so I'd rather not. Tell me what you were really thinking."

Koizumi's handsome face broke into a smile as he chuckled in a low voice that grated on my ears.

"Then I should tell you that the explanation I previously gave was true up to a point. However, the last part was different."

I kept my mouth shut.

"Keiichi approached the door with the knife stuck in his chest...Everything up to that point was true. So was the locking of the door by reflex. That was when the story diverged."

Koizumi motioned for me to sit down in a chair, but I ignored him.

"It appears that you've realized the truth. I must admit that I underestimated you."

"Just keep talking."

Koizumi shrugged.

"We rammed into the door and destroyed it. Or to be specific, myself, you, and Arakawa. And then the door was opened. Our momentum carried us inside."

I kept quiet as I motioned for him to keep going.

"You should already know the end result. Keiichi was standing right next to the door when it burst open and hit the front of his body. And the handle of the knife."

I tried to picture that scene in my mind.

"And consequently, the knife was driven into Keiichi's chest and led to his demise."

Koizumi sat back down on the bed and looked up at me provocatively.

"In other words, the culprits were..."

Koizumi smiled as he whispered to me, "Myself, you, and Arakawa."

I looked down at Koizumi. If I'd had a mirror, I could have seen the chilling look on my face. Koizumi didn't seem to care as he continued talking.

"Suzumiya also realized this truth, the way you did. That's why she stopped herself when she was about to tell us. She didn't accuse us of any wrongdoing. She may have wanted to protect her good friends."

Koizumi had a solemn look on his face. But I still couldn't accept what he was saying. My neocortex hadn't deteriorated to the point where I would be tricked by his second fake deduction.

"Hmph."

I snorted and glared at Koizumi.

"Sorry, but I don't trust you."

"What do you mean?"

"Your goal may have been to sell the second explanation with your tricky deduction, but you'll have to try harder if you want to fool me."

Didn't I sound pretty cool just now? I'll keep going.

"Just think about the fundamental problem here. As in focus

205

on the murder itself. Got it? There is no way that something like that could have happened under such convenient circumstances."

Now it was Koizumi's turn to silently motion me on.

"I don't know if the hurricane was a coincidence or Haruhi's doing, but it doesn't really matter in this case. The problem would be that we've got a dead body on our hands as a result."

I paused to lick my lips.

"You would probably claim that the whole thing happened because Haruhi wished for it. However, despite what she says, Haruhi does not actually wish for anyone to die. That should be obvious if you've watched her. Which means that this whole incident wasn't caused by Haruhi. And, are you listening? It wasn't a coincidence that we were here when it happened."

"Oh," said Koizumi. "So what does that mean?"

"The true culprit behind this incident...or actually this trip, the SOS Brigade summer camp, would be you. Am I wrong?"

Koizumi's smiling face froze for a few seconds as he was caught off guard. However—

A chuckling sound came from Koizumi's throat.

"You've got me. How did you know?"

As Koizumi said that, he looked at me with eyes that were the same as when we were in the literary club room.

I guess my brain tissue wasn't gray for no reason. I continued, feeling somewhat relieved. "Back when you asked Nagato for the body temperature of the corpse."

"What about that?"

"You used that temperature to estimate the time of death or whatever."

"Indeed, I did."

"Nagato can be very useful. As you should know, she can pretty much tell us anything. You should have asked Nagato for the estimated time of death instead of the body temperature. No, it wouldn't be an estimate. She could probably tell you the exact time of death now to the exact second."

"I see."

"If you had asked for the time of death, Nagato would have answered that he wasn't dead. Also, you never referred to Tamaru's body as a corpse."

"I was trying to be fair."

"There's still more. I'm actually an attentive person, though it may not seem that way. The interior side of the door to Keiichi's room. According to your explanation, the door hit the handle of the knife with a fair amount of force. Enough to drive a knife into a human body. If that much force had been involved, there should have been some kind of indentation on the door. But there wasn't. The door looked brand-new, without a scratch."

"What splendid powers of observation."

"And one more thing. It concerns Arakawa and Mori. The story that they hadn't even been here for a week yet. You said they were hired a week ago and that's when they came to this island, right?"

"That's right. Is there something odd about that?"

"There is. There definitely is. Your behavior was odd. Remember the first day we were here. What did you say when Arakawa and Mori came to pick us up when we got off the ferry?"

"Well, what did I say?"

" 'It's been quite some time.' Those were your words. Why would you say that? You said that this was your first time on this island. So this should have been the first time you ever met them. Why would you greet Arakawa and Mori as though you were already acquainted with them? Shouldn't that be impossible?"

Koizumi chuckled.

I took his laughter to be an open confession. All the tension left my body as I finally understood the whole picture, and Koizumi began to talk.

"That's right. This whole affair was a setup. A grand act. Though I didn't expect you to realize it."

"Don't underestimate me."

"Excuse me. However, I must admit that I was surprised. I had intended to reveal the truth at a later time, but I didn't expect to be caught so soon."

"Which means that Tamaru, Mori, and everyone else were all in on it? They're probably members of that 'Agency' thing, right?"

"That is correct. Pretty good acting for a bunch of amateurs, don't you think?"

The knife in the chest was a trick one with a retractable blade, the red bloodstain was actually paint, Keiichi was only pretending to be dead, of course, and the missing Yutaka had merely moved the cruiser to the other side of the island.

Koizumi revealed the truth in an easy manner.

"Why did you come up with this plan?"

"To ease Suzumiya's boredom. And to lessen our burden."

"What do you mean?"

"I'm pretty sure that I've already told you this. Basically, we were trying to provide Suzumiya with entertainment to prevent her from getting any strange ideas. For the time being, Suzumiya is focused on the current turn of events, is she not?"

"Except that Haruhi thinks we're the killers. Is that a good idea?"

After the presumed murder, Haruhi had been unusually quiet. She'd appeared to be deep in thought. Creepy as hell.

"Then I'll have to move up the schedule," Koizumi said. "According to our plan, we would return by ferry to the harbor on the mainland to find the four of them, Keiichi Tamaru and Yutaka, along with Arakawa and Mori, greeting us with smiles—that was the ending we'd prepared. Naturally, we would hide anything concerning the 'Agency' and stick to the story that they're my relatives."

So you actually had a surprise party planned.

I sighed. I hope Haruhi has a good sense of humor. If she gets seriously pissed, you'll have to deal with her. 'Cause I'll be long gone.

Koizumi winked at me as he smiled.

"That would be quite the predicament. I should probably apologize to her soon then. I shall go with Tamaru and everyone else to bow our heads in apology. I'm sure he's getting tired of playing a corpse."

I kept my mouth shut as I looked out the window.

I wondered how Haruhi would react. Would she go into a mad rage about being tricked, or would she just smile and laugh it off? Either way, she'll end up in a mental state that's easier to understand than the one she's in now.

Koizumi smiled wryly as he continued, "I had people ready to play the roles of detective and forensic expert, but it appears that those preparations will go to waste. In any case, I didn't expect such an uneventful ending. The original agenda included a search of the mansion as well as gathering evidence from the scene of the crime... It didn't work out too well."

That just shows that you didn't think this through enough.

As I looked up at the clouds, I wondered how clear the skies would be in a few hours.

In the end, Koizumi wasn't stripped of the title of vice brigade chief. The hurricane quickly disappeared and we took the ferry back under a bright, blue sky. Haruhi was in a good mood that lasted the entire trip up until we parted ways in front of the station. It's a good thing that Haruhi knows how to take a joke.

In return on the ferry trip back, Koizumi had to buy box lunches and canned juice for everybody. I felt that he'd gotten off pretty lightly.

Nagato, who probably knew what was going on from the beginning, showed no reaction. Asahina woke up to yell, "That was so mean!" and pout in an adorable manner, but once Koizumi and the Tamaru brothers along with the two servants bowed their heads in apology, she quickly said, "Ah, it's fine. Please don't worry about it!" I figured I should include that little episode in here.

Incidentally, Haruhi had made the following request when we were all lined up to take a picture on the deck of the ferry during the trip back to the mainland.

"I'll be counting on you for our winter camp, Koizumi. Come up with a better scenario this time. We'll be going to a mountain retreat. And there has to be a blizzard. You better provide an appropriately designed manor this time or I'll be mad. Yep. I can't wait!"

"Well...What to do?"

Koizumi turned to me for salvation, looking like a rookie German officer who'd received a direct order from the Führer himself to capture the Supreme Allied Commander with a single squad on the European Western Front during the waning years of World War II.

I looked at Koizumi the way you would look at a defender who had just made a beautiful shot into his own goal, during what had been a tied championship match up to that point, before speaking insincerely.

"Beats me. I'm also looking forward to it, Koizumi."

I assume that I can at least expect a solution that isn't so weak that even I could figure it out.

And so Haruhi won't be so bored with the ordinary to the point that she would cause extraordinary phenomena to happen.

AFTERWORD

I don't know the story behind the practice of including an afterword at the end of a book, but it's become as universally accepted as holes in Swiss cheese. Additionally, I should mention that I was told that I could write as many pages as I wanted for this section, an offer that would normally make me dance for joy, but I'll save that for a later opportunity. I would like to take this chance to write a few comments on each of the stories included in this book.

My overall impression will come across as "a year goes by in no time, but two months go by even faster," a no-brainer, so I hope that I don't bore you to death.

"The Boredom of Haruhi Suzumiya"

The namesake for this book was also the first printed edition of the SOS Brigade's exploits. I believe it appeared in *The Sneaker* around two months before "The Melancholy of Haruhi Suzumiya" was published.

Afterword

I was pretty worried about publishing a story about later events before the first book, but it appeared that I was the only person who harbored such doubts as nobody else questioned the idea, which was a big relief for me. After all, I wrote this story on the spur of the moment so I was worried about the quality, but in the end, there weren't any positive or negative comments that reached my ears so I just had to live with it.

Incidentally, I've only played baseball around ten times, as far as I can remember. I probably don't need to tell you about my exploits as a second baseman who couldn't catch a fly ball. I just now realized that I can't recall ever hitting the ball, which is quite a shock, albeit late in coming.

"Bamboo Leaf Rhapsody"
The original title was "The Confusion of Mikuru Asahina." However, there was some discussion about how it would be hard to recognize the series title so we ended up with this title. At the time, I didn't expect these short stories to be published on a regular basis, so I can vividly remember how horrified I was when I saw the words "to be continued in the next issue" on the last page when it appeared in the magazine.

Since I had a time traveler to work with, I felt that I was obligated to write a story about time travel, but there was a sense that this episode would foreshadow the next volume—which was my goal.

"Mysterique Sign"
Owing to extenuating circumstances, I believe that this story

was a personal best in terms of the time it took from idea to completion. I was considering what to put the group through, and the next thing I knew, this is what I ended up with. This was around the time when I started considering changing the title of the series to *Fight On, Nagato*, but I gave up on the idea since the story wouldn't go anywhere. Still, she appears to be the most effective character in the bunch. I have high expectations for her. Really, I'm counting on you, Nagato. By the way, what should I do about her glasses? Does she look better with them?

I had intended to give the computer society president some more action, but for now, I don't have any specific ideas so I can't really say how that will work out.

"Remote Island Syndrome"

I actually began writing this before "Mysterique Sign," and this story was supposed to appear in the magazine, but as I continued, it just kept getting longer and longer, so owing to various circumstances that were entirely my fault, it ended up as an extra story in this book. Which is why it boasts the highest page count in this volume as an extra story which was too long to run in the magazine and too short to publish as a stand-alone book. This episode gave me much to reflect on. I'm always thinking about how to work things out, but if thinking was all it took, everything would be so much easier. In fact, when I look back at my life, I can only count a few examples where something happened the way I wanted. And that is the reason my brain is in amoeba status now.

I wonder if someone might allow me to stay a week at a fancy resort on a remote island. I'm pretty sure I could at least serve as a witness. Though I'll probably spend the whole day sleeping.

And so, I was able to publish this third volume. I would like to express my gratitude to everyone who made it to this point. I would love to list everybody's name, position, and nickname, but the list would include all the readers out there, many of whom I do not know the names of, so I'll have to scrap the idea as there would be no end if I began. Instead, I can only offer my sincere appreciation.

I hope to see you again somewhere.

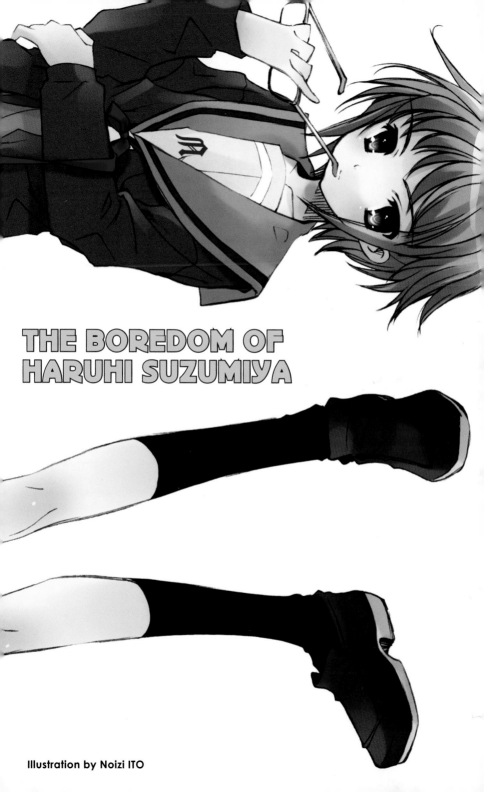

THE BOREDOM OF
HARUHI SUZUMIYA

Illustration by Noizi ITO

ASAHINA (BIG) POKED ASAHINA (SMALL)'S CHEEK.